Elam's chest was still bare except for the gun and holster.

Averting her eyes, she passed him, feeling him watch her as she applied sunscreen and then reclined on the yacht's sunbathing pad. Telling herself there was no reason to be nervous, she opened her book and started to read. That lasted all of thirty seconds.

He climbed onto the pad and reclined next to her, his mouth curved into a licentious grin.

"What are you reading?"

She showed him the cover.

"The Good Girl's Guide to Bad Men?"

"I caught my fiancé sleeping with someone else."

"And you think that book is going to help you avoid men like that?"

"I'll try anything once."

"Maybe you should try being alone for a while."

She eyed him from behind the security of her sunglasses, taking in his bare chest and gun. "Does that work for you?"

"I've never had a wom

"Have you ever had on the chance?"

Dear Reader,

Welcome to the second story in the ALL MCQUEEN'S MEN miniseries. In *The Secret Soldier,* I introduced you to Cullen McQueen, a tough and true former Delta Force soldier whose super-secret counterterror organization was nearly destroyed when his identity was exposed. But his stealth, determination and loyalty led him to emerge bigger and more powerful than ever in *Heiress Under Fire.*

Aside from just plain having a natural and persistent adoration for men, I love writing strong military heroes. Their bravery in combat, their intelligence in strategy, and their unrelenting, patriotic hearts inspire me. In a way, this miniseries is a tribute to their protectiveness and love of country and freedom.

So find a comfy place to curl up and spend a few hours discovering what Cullen's been up to. I hope you enjoy the journey as much as I did.

Jennifer

JENNIFER MOREY

Heiress Under Fire

Romantic
SUSPENSE

SILHOUETTE BOOKS

ISBN-13: 978-0-373-27648-6

HEIRESS UNDER FIRE

Recycling programs
for this product may
not exist in your area.

Printed in U.S.A.

Books by Jennifer Morey

Silhouette Romantic Suspense
The Secret Soldier #1526
Heiress Under Fire #1578

JENNIFER MOREY

has been creating stories since she fell in love with *The Black Stallion* by Walter Farley. She has a BS in geology from Colorado State University and is now an associate project manager for the spacecraft systems segment of a satellite imagery and information company. Jennie has received several awards for her writing, one that led to the publication of her debut novel, *The Secret Soldier.* She lives in Loveland, Colorado, with her yellow Lab and golden retriever.

To Katie Wheeler, whose happy ending was stolen by cancer. This happy ending is for her.

To all my friends at DigitalGlobe, you know who you are. Thank you for sharing this ride and putting up with my daydreaming. Sandra Kerns, Annette Elton, Julie Stevens, Susan LeDoux and Laura Leonard; thank you for being such awesome friends and keeping my stories and my characters honest and true. Jackie, my dearest, sweetest twin, I know there is a romance novel somewhere out there for you. I love you to pieces. Dad, your unabashed and lively promotional efforts will always make me smile.

And as always, to my mother, Joan Morey. She will forever be my deepest inspiration.

Chapter 1

Farren Gage removed a vacuum tube from the 1931 Atwater Kent radio she'd picked up at an auction a few days ago. Normally, digging her manicured fingers into a vintage piece like this made her feel relaxed. Not today. Not yesterday, either. Or the day before…

Putting the vacuum tube aside, she leaned back with a sigh on the creaky white dining-room chair, looking through the window. The ocean churned dark and turbulent under low, gray clouds. Steady rain had given way to wind today. She loved days like this, but all this idle time was going to drive her nuts.

She tapped her long fingernails on the old wood table. Maybe she shouldn't have quit her job yet. She missed the long drive to and from Bangor, Maine, where she worked. Coming home every night to Mount Desert Island and the little town of Bar Harbor had always given her a satisfying sense of peace. The road to her renovated farmhouse curved along the coast, offering a view of the Atlantic all the way to her gravel driveway. She should be exulting that she could retire at thirty-one and enjoy all this. Instead, she just felt…what was it?

Sad. And bitter.

She still couldn't understand why Carolyn and Jared Fenning had named her contingent beneficiary in their will. It seemed like a lifetime ago when she'd been so alone and scared, facing a childhood with foster parents who barely tolerated her. Jared hadn't liked kids and it had been easy enough for Carolyn to abandon her four-year-old girl for him. What kind of mother would do that and then leave her daughter a fortune after she and her husband croaked? Was it a gesture of guilt? Some kind of warped attempt at redemption? It only made Farren resent her mother more. Making her rich didn't replace face-to-face interaction. She felt cheated.

Looking down at the table, she caught sight of the itinerary she'd found when she'd gone to Fort Lauderdale to go through everything in Carolyn's big, gaudy house. She slid the paper closer. Something about it bothered her. Why had her mother planned to go to Bodrum, Turkey, and charter a yacht? It appeared her mother had planned to go by herself. Farren hadn't found an itinerary for Jared, and she thought it was peculiar that they'd killed each other after Carolyn had made the reservations. A little over a month ago, Jared shot Carolyn at their home, but she'd managed to shoot him, too. Jared had died faster, since she'd blasted his heart and he'd missed hers. Both died before help arrived. The lawyer who contacted Farren said the killings were the result of a domestic dispute. But she couldn't stop wondering if there was more—that the trip to Turkey had something to do with it. Had Carolyn been about to leave her husband and had he not wanted to let her go? Had they fought over that?

Farren studied the notes her mother had written on the itinerary. *International Marmaris Yacht Festival. Yacht = Lucky.* Was *Lucky* the name of a yacht that would be present at the festival in Marmaris, Turkey? Underneath the yacht's name, her mother had written *Saturday, May 14th, 8:00 a.m.* Had her mother planned to meet someone then? It seemed that way. She was scheduled to sail to Marmaris from Bodrum the day before that, and the flight had been ticketed the same day she was killed. Was that significant?

The telephone rang.

Farren got up from the chair and went into her hardwood-floored kitchen with white cabinets and tile countertops. She picked up the phone from a hanging wood shelf. It was a wireless caller, she saw from the display.

"Hello?"

"You have a beautiful home," a male voice said in accented English. He sounded Arabic, but his English was good.

"Who is this?"

"Alone and away from town. On such a large parcel of land," he said without acknowledging her. "How easy it would be to kill you."

Her heart burst into frightened beats. Was this man stalking her? "Look, this isn't funny. If you're—"

"Listen carefully," he growled, changing trigger-quick from mock admiration to anger. "Soon you will have wire instructions. You will follow them or I will come into your pretty house and kill you. Scream all you like. I doubt even your neighbor will hear you."

A sick feeling twisted in her stomach. "What is this about? I don't know anything about any wire instructions and I don't owe anyone any money."

"You will pay, or you will die. I know where you live. I know who your friends are. I know everything about you. Go to the police and you will not live to see another day. I will have my money, or I will have your life."

She moved past the table and looked through the front window. No strange car was parked in front of her house. No one walked along the street.

"Who are you?" she demanded.

"Jared Fenning owed me money. You have it now. You will wire transfer three million dollars to an account once I provide the number. Do you understand?"

"Tell me who you are. Why did Jared owe you money?" she frantically asked.

"I will kill you if you do not do as I say."

"But—"

The line went dead.

Farren heard her own breathing. The clock on the wall near the refrigerator tick-tocked. Her hand trembled, still holding the phone to her ear. She finally lowered it.

The doorbell rang and her entire body jolted.

Putting the phone down, she straightened the long-sleeved denim shirt she wore over her black cotton sundress and walked into the living room on her way to the door. She peered through the peephole. No one was there. She caught a movement and saw a young boy hurrying onto his bicycle and riding down her gravel driveway.

Farren opened the door. A box sat on her white wood porch, a few feet from her pink-painted toenails. She crouched to pick up the box, then lifted her head. The boy disappeared down the road.

What was this all about? Apprehension made her wary, but she took the box inside and shut the door. Back in the dining room, she put the box on the table next to the old radio. Finding a knife, she sliced the packing tape and opened the box.

A piece of paper lay folded inside. It was on top of something wrapped in red tissue paper. She lifted the piece of paper and unfolded it. Wire instructions were typed on the page.

Dread plunged through her system and pumped her heart faster. She looked inside the box. Parting the tissue paper, she saw a blood-soaked scarf bunched underneath. She recognized the printed daisies along the edges. Her neighbor's scarf. It used to be white. Delphie Sinclair had just worn it yesterday.

"No." Farren dropped the paper and ran to the front door, sicker than ever. Flinging it open, she raced across the lawn toward her neighbor's house. She could see it from here. A pale yellow, white-trimmed two-story house. Sweet and innocent. Just like Delphie.

I know everything about you.

"Delphie!" she yelled. That man must have been watching her. Seen her with Delphie.

Passing a couple of apple trees, she made it to Delphie's flower-bordered lawn and charged onto the porch. She gripped the handle. It was locked. She pounded on the door. "Delphie!" She pounded again. "Oh, God."

The lock unlatched and the door opened.

Delphie stood there with a wrinkled brow creased deep in a frown. "What in heaven's name is the matter with you?"

Farren couldn't breathe deep enough. "Oh—my—God." She stepped toward Delphie and took her into her arms and started crying.

"What's wrong, Farren?"

Farren leaned back. "Are you all right?" She blinked her

eyes clear and sniffled as she searched Delphie's body for signs of injury.

"Of course I'm all right. Why wouldn't I be?"

"Has anyone been here to see you?"

"No. Farren, what's going on?"

Farren entered the house, wiping her eyes with an unsteady hand. She made her way into the kitchen and sat in a white chair at the table, still shaky. Delphie's kitchen looked similar to hers, except she'd painted her walls yellow where Farren's were a more earthy mushroom shade.

"Someone just threatened me."

A teakettle began to whistle. Delphie went to the stove and turned the burner down. "What?"

Farren noticed the woman's socks, one green, the other pink. One reached higher on her calf than the other. She still wore her white terry-cloth robe and big cream-colored furry slippers. Affection for the old woman worked to calm her nerves a little.

"A man called and demanded three million dollars," she said. "He said he's going to kill me if I don't make a wire transfer to an account."

Delphie poured hot water over a tea bag in a cup and brought it to Farren, her long gray hair falling forward as she leaned over the table.

"Do you think he knows about your inheritance?"

"Oh, yeah. He knows."

"Then he must be some crazy who's trying to scare you to swindle some money. Change your number and get a good security system."

Farren shook her head. "He said Jared owed him money."

Delphie went to get her own cup of tea. "He knew the Fennings?"

Farren shivered and held the warm cup with both hands.

Now more than ever she suspected Carolyn and Jared's deaths had not resulted from a mere domestic dispute. Had Carolyn discovered something and that's what made her husband want to kill her? And was it connected to the yacht in Marmaris?

Delphie sat across from her, setting the cup on the table. "Did he say why Jared owed him money?"

Farren shook her head again.

"And you're sure this wasn't some kind of loon after a piece of your inheritance?"

"Yes. He was serious. Jared owed him money and now he wants me to pay." And his refusal to tell her why made her skin crawl. Was her inheritance dirty money?

"You should go to the police," Delphie said.

Go to the police and you will not live to see another day.

What would happen if she went to the police despite the stranger's warning? She was afraid to try. But she couldn't hand over three million without knowing what it was for.

"I don't know what to do."

"Call the police."

"I'm not so sure that's a good idea right now. The man who threatened me knows where I live. I think he's watching me." She rubbed her arms against the shiver that chilled her. "He had a scarf of yours delivered to my door. It was covered in blood."

Delphie's mouth dropped open and she gasped. "Are you sure it was mine?"

"It was the white one you wore yesterday. It had little pink daisies on the edges." At least they'd been pink before the scarf was doused in blood.

Delphie froze. "I was looking for that this morning." She paused in thought. "Someone broke into my house and took it!"

"To make a point."

Rising from her chair, Delphie marched toward the phone hanging on the wall. "We have to call the police."

"No." Farren sprang to her feet and went after her. She took the phone from her aging hand and met vibrant blue eyes that defied her eighty years. "No."

"Farren…"

"I have a bad feeling about this."

"All the more reason to call for help."

"What if I go to the police and there's nothing they can do? The caller warned me not to go to the police. What if I do and instead of bloodying another scarf, he comes after me?"

I will have my money, or I will have your life.

"You can't handle this on your own."

"I can't go to the police. Not yet."

"Then what are you going to do?"

Farren thought of her mother's itinerary and the notes she'd written on it. Carolyn's flight was scheduled to leave tomorrow. If she canceled the reservations and made some of her own, what would she find after boarding a yacht in Bodrum and sailing to Marmaris just like her mother had planned? And when she reached Marmaris, what would she find on a yacht called *Lucky?* Had her mother intended to meet someone she hadn't wanted her husband to know about? Whoever Farren found aboard *Lucky* might be able to give her insight into what led to her mother's death. Dare she go? What if that someone turned out to be the one threatening her? But how? That someone was here, watching her.

She looked at Delphie. "I need you to go to your sister's in Chicago."

"I was planning to go next month."

"Go tomorrow. I'll pay for the change."

"Why? What are you going to do?"

"I'm going to Turkey."

"Turkey... What? Why would you do that?" She paused. "Is this about your mother's trip to Bodrum?"

She'd already told her about the notes. "It might be the only way I can find answers."

"Farren, you're an electrical engineer, not an investigator. You could get hurt."

"I won't do anything I don't feel is safe. I just want to talk to whomever my mother was going to meet in Marmaris. Besides, it might be good if I disappear for a while." It might be good if they both disappeared. If they weren't here, no one could hurt them.

"You don't know if your mother was going to meet anyone in Marmaris," Delphie said.

"I have a feeling she was." It was the only thing she had to go on.

Delphie didn't respond, but her eyes said it all.

"Don't worry about me. If nothing turns up in Marmaris, I'll at least have some time to myself. No one will expect me to travel all the way to Turkey." She wondered if her mother had thought the same.

"You might get more than you can handle," Delphie muttered.

"No one will know I'm there. I'll look like just another tourist. Besides, I really could use some time away. Look at all the awful men I've been choosing lately. I'm too impulsive. Too impatient. I rush into things with a man before I can see how wrong he is for me. Look what happened with Payton. Obviously, I'll settle for anyone as long as he can procreate. I need to figure out why I keep doing that and stop it."

"You could do that here."

"I've been engaged four times," Farren went on. Talking relaxed her and that caller had made her nervous. Now that the excitement had passed, she couldn't stop herself. "I must never have gotten over the way I was raised. I never felt like I was part of a real family and I always wanted one. And the older I get the more I panic I'll never have one. Payton came along and seemed to like me. He was a decent man."

Delphie's eyebrows lifted.

"Okay, I *thought* he was decent. That's the problem, don't you see? I think anyone is decent as long as they want me. I'm *desperate*." She had to be. "Why couldn't I see Payton never really wanted me? I never even loved him. I just wanted him to marry me and get me pregnant. I would have ended up miserable and lonely and unloved. I should have known better. I should have known he was bad for me when he made fun of my radio collection. What's wrong with collecting old radios? Why did he think that was so silly? I got straight A's in college but you would never know it. I'm as stupid as they come with men. Blonde jokes? That's me." She held up some of her long blond hair for emphasis.

"All right." Delphie held her hand up against Farren's unending chatter. "I'll go to my sister's." She sighed in exasperation. "When you get going like that, I know there's no arguing with you. It's either agree or listen to you talk for the next two hours."

Farren smiled. "You will? You'll go?"

"And you aren't stupid. You just haven't found the right man yet."

"What if I never do?"

"Payton is a politician. You were too honest for him. You're right, your only problem is you aren't patient. You need to *wait* for the right one. Don't leap into engagements just because someone asks."

"Yeah, I know I have no sense when it comes to men."

Delphie angled her head and contemplated Farren with warmth in her eyes. "Just stop looking for it. Don't try so hard. It'll happen when it happens."

Farren wasn't so sure. "I wish it was that simple."

Delphie gave her hand a squeeze. "Be careful in Turkey. Stay out of trouble, okay?"

"I'm not going to look for a man, so that should be no problem."

Elam Rhule stepped out of the car and thanked the driver. Crystalline blue sky and towering mountain peaks all but swallowed Roaring Creek, Colorado. Winters had to be brutal here. Not a soul stirred in the early May chill. He glanced across the street as the car drove away. A sign above the door of an old brick building read Rock Miser Books & Coffee.

For the life of him, he couldn't imagine why a man with Cullen McQueen's reputation would headquarter his top secret counter-terror organization in a town like this. Where the hell was he? Bedrock?

He started up the narrow sidewalk toward the front door of RC Mountaineering. The two-story building almost had as much charm as the bookstore, minus frilly white curtains and shutters trimming the windows. The front door opened and Cullen appeared.

"It's about time you got here."

"My flight was delayed," Elam said. He'd flown to a small airstrip just outside town. "Sorry to keep your driver waiting."

Cullen stepped aside to let him enter. The main room

and what once must have been a kitchen was full of climbing gear, backpacks, camping equipment and other backcountry paraphernalia. To his left, stairs led up to the second level.

Behind a checkout counter to his left, Odelia Frank spoke into a phone. Her dark eyes rolled over to see him, strands of equally dark hair deceptively sexy and feminine, framing her striking face. She winked at him. He smiled. Now there was a woman who did not fit small-town life. He wondered how much longer the tough ex–Army operations captain would last up here.

"You've been talking to your boyfriend for an hour," Cullen told her as he led Elam toward a door across the room. "I'm going to send you the bill."

Odie flipped him the bird and turned her back, leaning a shapely hip against the counter. If Elam didn't know she was seeing someone, he'd have already had her in bed.

Chuckling, Cullen entered a code into a keypad next to the door.

"You afraid Fred Flintstone is going to see us?" Elam asked as he followed him down a narrow flight of stairs.

At the bottom, Cullen turned to look back, not amused—if his expression was any clue. He had no sense of humor when it came to fighting terrorism, a trait Elam respected more than his six-foot-five powerhouse of a boss knew.

"Sorry. I just didn't expect this office to be so—" Elam looked around the simply decorated basement that had been finished into an office "—small."

He sat in one of two old wood chairs before the desk, watching Cullen do the same in a more comfortable one behind the desk. Catching sight of a photograph next to a flat-screen computer monitor, he gained a little insight into the location of Cullen's headquarters. A beautiful redhead with stunning green eyes smiled above the head of a baby girl who had eyes just like her. No doubt that's what had drawn him here.

"Don't let the image of fatherhood fool you," Cullen said.

Elam turned from the photograph. "It doesn't." He'd read all the press over Sabine O'Clery's rescue. At the time he'd shaken his head and marveled at how a man could be so careless, losing his head over a woman like that, future wife or not. But *careless* was not a word anyone could attach to Cullen. He'd brought his company back from ashes, restructured and renamed and relocated. Tactical Executive Security, or TES as the company was called now, did far more than assess infrastructure security for the government. The mountaineering shop was only a guise for the locals in Roaring Creek.

"I guess I just forgot you were married," Elam said.

Cullen breathed a single laugh. "I can see why."

Elam raised his brow.

"I was a lot like you once," he explained. "You think having a family can't happen to you, so you put it in the back of your mind."

Elam forced himself to smile. "Give me a woman who doesn't bolt because she's tired of wondering if I'll come home alive, and I'll keep her."

"You've met a lot of women who bolt?"

"One was enough." And he didn't want to talk about this anymore. His one attempt at marriage had ended in tragedy, adding to a list of them. He wasn't eager to try again.

Cullen's expression sobered and Elam knew what he was thinking. He knew all about his past. About how he'd awakened to television reports of an airplane exploding into the World Trade Center. About how he'd waited for word that his severely depressed mother was all right when a deeper part already knew she was gone, taking the last vestiges of his family with her.

"You said you heard from Osman Alfandari," Elam said to get the conversation back to business.

Cullen nodded. "He has news of a growing cell developing just outside Bodrum. We've identified the leader."

"And you want me to go in and take him out."

"He's not on anybody's radar and it will take too long to put him there. We have a narrow window of opportunity. I want him stopped before he gets dangerous. You're my best sniper and you can work alone. I also trust you not to get killed."

His boss did have a fierce streak when it came to losing his men. "I'm touched," he quipped. "What's my target's name?"

"Ameen Al-Jabbar. He's been nosing around Bodrum. Checked in at the Marina Vista Hotel yesterday and booked a week. I'd like to put a crimp in any plans he might have of car bombing a busy tourist attraction."

"You think he's scoping out a target?"

"Osman talked to a man who was in contact with one of Ameen's followers. They're planning more than one hit. Bodrum looks like the first."

So, if Elam took out Ameen, it would stall, if not stop, the group's plans and give TES more time to finish them off.

"When do I leave?"

"This afternoon. Commercial. So you look like a tourist. You'll fly back to Denver today and depart for Turkey from there."

"What about equipment?"

"Osman will meet you at the airport. He'll have everything you need."

Elam took the e-ticket Cullen handed him and stood. "You've made this easy for me."

"There's nothing easy about killing."

No, but he'd had plenty of practice. He slipped the e-ticket into the inside pocket of his leather jacket and turned. Killing was a job to him. He did it to make a difference, and he never missed.

Chapter 2

It had been a long flight into Bodrum yesterday and Farren was tired, but anxiety had kept her from getting much sleep. She couldn't believe it had only been two days ago that she'd gotten that scary call. Running her hand along the rail, she moved toward the bow of *Haven,* the yacht she'd chartered. The crew hadn't come back yet and the captain had said he needed to go into town before their scheduled departure. She had the yacht all to herself. She was pretty sure the captain had made up an excuse to get away from her. He seemed to have trouble keeping his eyes open when she talked. It happened sometimes. Delphie once told her she could suck the energy out of an evangelist.

Hearing a boat approach, she looked toward the stern but couldn't see anything. The boat engine died. The crew must have returned from shore. They were moored close to the docks of Bodrum Marina.

She sighed and tried to let her surroundings relax her. Turquoise water lapped the sides of the yacht. Classic architecture studded the shoreline, the sprawling Castle of St. Peter drawing her eye. The majestic structure was now a museum, and she'd spent a good portion of the morning taking in ancient artifacts and the history that accompanied them. This afternoon they'd sail to Marmaris. Then she'd have a day before the festival began and she could search for the yacht called *Lucky*. Hopefully someone on board could tell her why a man was threatening her for three million dollars.

Trailing her hand along the rail again, she moved toward the stern. Seeing a dinghy in the water, she wondered why no one had lifted it onto the *Haven* yet. Coming closer, she saw that it wasn't even tied to the yacht. Just then the muffled rumble of the yacht engine started. She hadn't seen the captain return. He'd taken an inflatable dinghy. Her brow tightened with the thought.

The yacht lurched into motion. Farren grabbed on to the railing to keep from losing her balance. The vessel turned to sea. Pretty soon, the sound of water spraying grew louder. Her hair began to whip around in the breeze. The dinghy and marina grew smaller as the yacht sailed farther to sea.

Why were they going so fast? And where was the crew? She should have seen someone by now. Her heart picked up a few extra beats.

She used the rail to make her way to the bow, looking up toward the flybridge. A man with dark hair and eyes and a trimmed beard maneuvered the vessel. Not the captain. Not a crewman. He looked down and saw her.

Who was that? Her pulse shot into rapid flight. What was he doing aboard this yacht? She was afraid she already knew.

She searched the deck for anyone else. There was no

one. She looked back at the flybridge. The man was gone. He reemerged portside along the rail, striding toward her, pulling a knife from a holder hidden by his hanging shirt. He had a piece of rope in his other hand.

Choking back a scream, Farren stumbled into a run, racing down the other side of the yacht. Reaching the stern, she pulled open the salon door and ran into the main cabin on the vessel. Footsteps pounded behind her. The man grabbed her wrist. She yanked it free, but the movement caused her to lose her balance. She stumbled and fell onto her hands. The man tossed the rope onto the couch to her left, and then knelt on one knee. Before she could get away, he gripped a handful of her hair and pulled her back against him. She felt the knife under her chin. Stark terror ripped through her.

"Please," she begged, hating that she had. "Don't."

He said something in a language she didn't understand. Oh, God. Her mind raced with panic. Gripping her arm, he hauled her to her feet and forced her to face him. The point of the knife now pressed against her throat. She tipped her head as far back as she could to ease the pressure. The angle allowed her to see his gaze slide down the front of her. She still wore the silk shorts and blouse outfit from her excursion to shore. Thankfully she hadn't changed into a swimsuit. That didn't seem to matter to him. When his eyes lifted and met hers, a weight of dread sank through her. Cold, dark lust stared back at her.

She felt her body begin to tremble. A whimper escaped despite her struggle to control her fear. The man gave her a rough shove and she fell onto a chair adjacent to the couch.

"Do not move," he said in English.

She sat frozen, staring at the shiny blade he now held in front of her nose.

He leaned to her right and retrieved the rope. Putting the knife on the top of a shelf next to the couch, he caught her wrists. She tried to pull away from his hold, but he wrapped the rope around her wrists with quick, strong hands. When he let go to reach for the knife, she scrambled off the chair and tried to crawl away from him on her knees. He took a handful of hair and yanked, slamming her against the chair, then raised his hand and slapped her hard. She fell to her right, hitting her head on the edge of the shelving. Dizzy, she moaned, feeling blood trickle from a cut. She had to stay coherent in order to think of a way out of this situation. But what could she do? He had a knife and she was trapped on a yacht with him.

Grabbing her chin, he forced her to look at him.

"Do not move or I will kill you."

His voice sounded different from the one who'd called her. Higher. Not as deep. Maybe this wasn't related to the threat.

"Who are you? What do you want?" she asked.

"You should not have come here," he said. "Now you will do as you were told."

Definitely related. The man who'd threatened her must have had her followed and sent this one after her. To what? Kidnap her? Force her to perform the wire transfer? If so, maybe she wouldn't be killed right away. But once the transfer was complete...what then?

"Do not move." The man stood, taking his knife with him as he left the salon. Long seconds later, she felt the yacht turn and pick up speed.

She used her teeth to work the knot in the rope. She couldn't wait here like this. She had to find a way to defend herself—had to take control of the yacht and find help before the man took her wherever it was he was heading. A sob broke from her. She didn't know if she was tough enough to fight him. Her foster parents' son had always teased her because she couldn't fight worth a darn.

The rope loosened. She pulled with her teeth until her hands slipped free. Heart flying, she spared a quick glance at the salon door before running to the kitchen. She found a butcher knife in one of the drawers. The thought of using it terrified her beyond comprehension. She couldn't picture herself plunging it into the man's chest. How hard would it be to bury it in his body? What if he deflected all her attempts? What if he stabbed her instead?

Another sob broke from her as she ran through the salon. She feared she was too loud. Panic engulfed her as she made it to her cabin, closed the door and locked it. Holding the knife in front of her so tight her hands felt numb, she backed away from the door and stared at it, waiting for it to crash open.

Shaking, she found her purse and took out her cell. No service. She wished she would have thought to rent a satellite phone. Then she could have at least called the marina for help.

Stumbling across the cabin, she entered the adjoining bathroom. In case the knife wasn't enough, she wanted to find whatever she could to use as backup. Hairspray. Toenail clippers. High-heeled shoes. Placing the objects around the room, careful to note and commit to memory where each one was, she faced the door and waited.

Farren lost track of the minutes that passed, but finally the yacht began to slow. There was a series of sputters and lurches. Then nothing. The engine died. With sickening clarity, she remembered the captain telling her they would need fuel before leaving for Marmaris.

"No," she whispered with renewed panic. Her heart hammered faster. "This can't be happening."

Footsteps sounded above her head. She followed them toward the stern. They fell out of earshot. But a few seconds later, she heard something in the salon.

A few wrenching sobs overwhelmed her struggle to remain quiet. Her eyes strained wide as she saw the door handle move. When the man discovered it locked, he began kicking.

Farren screamed and looked around the cabin. Could she break the window? She didn't think so. And it was too small anyway. Crying harder, fighting her fear, she listened to the door begin to splinter. A horrible rush of terror coursed through her.

The lock broke and the door crashed in. He stepped inside, eyes feral with anger.

"Stay away from me." Her mouth was cottony and dry from taking so many panting breaths.

"You were not to move." He came toward her, eyeing the knife and the rest of her body. He didn't have his knife. At least, he hadn't removed it from under his shirt.

"Stay back!" She tripped over the corner of the bed. At the wall, she had nowhere else to go.

He stalked toward her until he was within reach. She swung the knife. His hand snaked for her wrist, almost clasped it, but she yanked away and swung again, this time catching the blade on his chest. He grunted and his face darkened into a menacing scowl. He backhanded her before she saw it coming. The force of the blow sent her falling toward the bed. She used the momentum to crawl to the other side, stumble onto the floor and then run for the door. He caught her before she reached it. She kicked and punched and swung the knife. But he grabbed hold of her hand and squeezed. She yelped in pain and held on to the knife as long as she could. To her horror, it fell to the carpeted floor. He eased his grip and she pulled free, bending for the knife. He used his foot to shove it away. She wouldn't reach it before he caught her again.

Rushing to the table beside the bed, she fumbled with the container of hairspray. When she turned, the man was there.

She sprayed his eyes, pumping the nozzle as fast as she could. With a shout, he wiped his eyes.

Farren ran for the door, snatching the toenail clippers from the dresser on her way. Just as she made it out of the cabin, the man grasped some of her hair and yanked. She lost her balance and they both fell to the floor of the salon with grunts. She'd purposefully left the clippers open, and now the pointed file was between her fisted fingers. He rolled on top of her, straddling her hips, taking a handful of her silk top and ripping it down the front.

She hit him in the face with her artificial claw.

"Ahh!" he yelled. Blood sprouted from the puncture she'd made.

Encouraged, she started pummeling him again and again. He blocked her swings and grabbed her hand, squeezing until she yelped again and let go of the clippers. They fell to the floor beside her.

He went still and looked toward the doorway of the salon.

Farren wiggled beneath him. Was that a motorboat she heard? Had the crew come to rescue her? The man looked down at her with another angry scowl and arched his arm for another backhand.

"No!" She used her forearm to block him.

Instead of fighting her, he rose to his feet, grabbing her by the hair again and taking her with him. She fought, yelling in pain, kicking his shins as he forced her out of the salon and onto the deck. He yanked hard on his tether. She kicked again, then turned her head and tried to bite him. Near the stern, he hauled her up against him and put the knife to her throat. Only then did she realize he'd taken it from his holster.

She stopped breathing. Sick dread flooded her. Would he slice her throat before she made the wire transfer? She spotted another man crouched on the swim deck, poised and still, aiming a pistol. "Drop the knife," he said. He sounded uncompromising.

"I will kill her," her captor said.

"You'll be dead before that. Drop it."

The knife pressed harder against Farren's skin. With a pathetic whimper, she struggled to force her attacker's hand away from her throat.

The man on the swim deck slowly straightened, thick, dark hair waving in a slight breeze. He was a towering man with big shoulders and unwavering light-colored eyes. He climbed the stairs one step at a time, stopping on the main deck, his aim never faltering. He didn't seem ruffled at all. There was a chilling certainty about him.

Appearing to have sensed the same thing, her attacker hissed something in what she guessed was Arabic and gave her a shove. She stumbled right into the big man. Her heart raced with adrenaline as he caught her seconds before he fired his gun.

Her attacker grunted, blood sprouting on his shirt at his shoulder, as he ran down a second set of stairs leading to the swim deck. The big man steadied her as she tried to regain her footing. His body felt rock-hard and immovable against hers. Her attacker jumped into the motorboat the man holding her had used to get here and sped away from the yacht.

The man let go as he moved to the rail, methodical and unrelenting. He fired twice. Her attacker's body jerked and fell against the boat wheel before going limp and slumping out of sight. The boat kept speeding away.

Farren lifted a shaking hand and touched the base of her throat where her pulse thudded wildly. She heard her rapid breathing and felt light-headed with residual fear.

The man standing at the stern rail lifted his shirt and tucked the gun into a holster strapped to his bare skin, letting the shirt fall back into place. Turning, he faced her. He wore jeans with a white cotton, short-sleeved, button-up shirt that showed off his tanned and muscular arms.

"Are you all right?" he asked.

She lowered her hand. Her entire body trembled, but otherwise she was fine. She gave him a shaky nod.

"If you hadn't come when you did…" She shuddered with the thought. "That man was so strong and I didn't know what he was going to do. But then I heard you approach and, oh, my God, you have no idea how scared I was. I thought you were the crew coming back. They went ashore before our scheduled departure and I stayed on the yacht and…I wish I would have gone to shore with them. Then none of this would have happened and—"

The big man passed her and climbed the stairs next to the salon entrance.

Was he ignoring her? He headed for the stairs leading to the upper deck. She lost sight of him until he reappeared on the flybridge. She watched him work the controls in an attempt to start the yacht. No engine sounded. He tried the radio next. It must not have worked because he slammed his palms on the instrument panel before turning away and leaving the flybridge. He disappeared until she saw him step onto the main deck and stop at the edge of the aft deck.

In the distance the speedboat still moved away, beginning to turn to the right without anyone guiding the wheel.

Farren wondered how long it would take for it to run out of fuel and begin to just drift.

The man headed toward the bow. She started to follow on unsteady feet, then stopped. She didn't know him or his purpose. Why was he here? He'd saved her, but not knowing anything about him made her nervous.

As waves lapped gently against the yacht, the sound calming, she held the rail while her pulse finally began to slow and she was able to breathe normally. Moments later, the man reappeared, coming back toward her. Dark chocolate hair accentuated pale blue eyes. The white shirt conformed to his impressive chest.

"Is there a dinghy aboard this yacht?" he asked, stopping before her.

"The crew took it. I told you they went to shore. We were moored near the docks and they said they were going to get supplies. There was an inflatable dinghy, but the captain took that one to take care of something in town. But I'm sure he's noticed his yacht is missing by now. Someone will come looking for us. They probably already are. I mean, it's been—"

"Are there any others?" He cut her off.

She frowned at his rudeness. "Any other what?"

"Dinghies."

"Oh. I don't think so." She put her hand on her churning stomach. She felt worn out from fighting the man who'd commandeered her yacht.

The man's gaze traveled from her stomach up to her chest. She looked down at her lacy bra and exposed cleavage and pulled the ruined shirt together.

"Did he hurt you?" he asked in a less demanding tone.

"No."

"Looks like he did." He reached over and fingered her hair.

The drying blood in her hair reminded her that the man who'd taken over her yacht had bashed her head.

"Who are you?" she asked.

"Elam Rhule."

"Were you chasing that man?"

"I better take a look at your head," he said instead of answering.

She followed him into the salon. "It seemed like you were chasing him." And she wanted to know why.

Still, he didn't answer.

"Are you some kind of cop?" she asked anyway. "What are you doing in Turkey? You talk as if you're from the United States. Where are you from?" He didn't say anything, but she realized she hadn't really given him a chance.

He led her to the bathroom and started opening cabinets.

"Who was he? A drug dealer?" This time she paused to give him time to answer. He didn't. "He had creepy eyes. As if there was no life in them. He scared me like you would not believe. Look at me." She held up her trembling hand. "I'm still shaking."

Turning on the water, Elam looked at her while he kept a finger under the stream. "Do you always talk this much?"

"Do you always ignore people when they ask you questions?"

Dampening a piece of gauze, he moved close to her and began washing the injured area of her head. She looked at his face. She'd never seen one so rugged before. The man oozed masculinity. A blocky jaw contrasted with sensual lips, but not in a way that detracted from his manliness. Rather, the mix between soft and hard enhanced the effect. And those eyes. Fringed by thick lashes, they were the color of pool water.

"Have you ever seen the original *Sniper* movie?" she asked.

His gaze rolled down to look at her.

"You remind me of Tom Berenger in that movie," she said when he didn't answer. "Except your jaw is wider and your hair is longer. Darker, too." Sexier. "And your eyes are really blue."

He stopped washing her cut and observed her with those magnificent eyes.

"You're probably taller, too," she went on despite her fluttering nerves. "Bigger." Okay, so maybe he wasn't all that much like Tom Berenger. It was just the way his eyes glowed that made her think of the comparison.

"Hollywood always makes actors seem so much bigger than they really are," she said. "So many of them act like big tough guys, when really they're nothing but short little wimps." She wrinkled her nose in distaste. "I don't like that."

When he turned and opened the medicine cabinet, she tried not to notice his butt. It was too hard not to in those jeans.

"Aren't you going to tell me who that man was?" she asked.

He faced her again. "Take these."

She looked down at his hand and saw three aspirin. Plucking them from his palm, she looked up at his ruggedly handsome face and waited for an answer. When none came, she left the bathroom and headed for the galley. Opening the refrigerator, she took out a bottle of water.

"What's your name?" he asked as she swallowed the last pill.

"Farren Gage," she answered. "Why were you chasing that man?" This time she wasn't going to let him not answer.

He contemplated her, taking his time as he considered

whether to oblige. She doubted anyone could force him to do anything.

"I came here to kill him," he finally said.

"You came to Bodrum to kill a man?"

Nothing changed on his face. He didn't say anything, either. He had a scary way about him, and yet…she wasn't afraid of him.

"Why?" she asked.

He just kept looking at her.

"How did you know he came aboard this yacht?" she pressed.

"I saw him boat to where you were moored and climb onto it."

"You followed him? Is that why he commandeered this yacht? Because you were chasing him?" She wanted to find out how much he knew about the man.

"He didn't know I was following him."

Because he'd come to kill the man. "Why were you?"

"Why did he choose this yacht?" he asked.

Whoa. This guy didn't miss a thing. But she didn't think he knew the man had come to kidnap her. "I don't know," she lied. She knew nothing about him and wasn't sure how much she should say about the threatening phone call.

His gaze floated over her face, her mouth and her eyes, where they stayed. She felt interrogated without words. Did he know she wasn't being truthful? It seemed that way. But he didn't force the issue. After meeting her eyes a few seconds longer, he turned and left the galley.

Elam rooted through the refrigerator for something to eat. The sun had set and he was starving but he hated cooking. Everything in this fridge would take too much effort to prepare. Figures, a rich lady all by herself on a yacht wouldn't have any pot pies or pizza. From the salon, an Avril Lavigne song started to play. This was the third time Farren had played the same CD. It was starting to grate on him. At least she wasn't talking his ear off. The woman was tireless.

A light came on behind him. He straightened and turned.

Long blond hair still damp from a shower hung to Farren's fantastic breasts. Her amber eyes were soft and magnetizing. She'd put on white cotton shorts and a black-and-white sleeveless top. No shoes. She looked delicate standing there. Soft. Feminine. Not a drop of military blood in her.

He'd sworn off women like her the day his wife walked out on him. So why did he like looking at her so much?

"No luck with the engine?" she asked, moving to the counter where he'd put a bag of chips and anything else that wouldn't require a fuss.

"We're out of fuel."

"The radios are smashed, too," she said, popping a chip into her mouth.

"I saw that." Ameen Al-Jabbar had not only disabled the radios in the flybridge and the pilothouse, he'd pitched the radar deflector and Emergency Position Indicating Radio Beacon overboard. Another peculiarity. Why had he chosen this yacht and destroyed all the communication capability? Had he feared Farren would try to attract authorities before he got away in one piece?

Elam had had him in his crosshairs before a woman and child had blocked his aim. That's when he left his position in a hotel balcony window and followed him, leaving his sniper rifle behind and taking his pistol. At the marina, his target had gotten away in the crowd. A few minutes later, he'd spotted him motoring away in a small boat. He found a speedboat and followed.

Ameen hadn't been in a hurry. He hadn't looked behind him. He hadn't seen Elam in the speedboat. That meant he had deliberately climbed aboard *Haven*. Had he known Farren would be there? He hadn't seen Elam following him. There was no reason for him to run. She said she didn't know why the man had hijacked her yacht, but the flicker in her eyes when she'd denied it made him wonder. Why would she lie about that? She was a blond, flowery thing who'd probably never held a gun in her entire life. It didn't make sense that she'd be tangled up with the likes of Ameen. The contrast between the two was so extreme it almost made him laugh.

Farren touched the can of tuna sitting next to a can of creamed corn. "What were you planning to make with this?"

"Dinner."

"Tuna and creamed corn?" She wrinkled her nose. "Maybe you should let me do the cooking."

"You cook?"

She sent him an unappreciative look.

"Sorry. You don't strike me as the Betty Crocker type."

"You should really try to open your mind a little."

He grinned at the sass coming from such sexy lips. Leaning a hip against the counter, he watched her put a frying pan on the stove and start mixing flour and seasoning in a bowl.

"Did you see that movie *Six Days Seven Nights?*" she asked while she worked.

"Is it a chick flick?"

"A pilot and a magazine editor get stranded on this island. The pilot perceives the editor all wrong, like she's too soft and pampered to handle the wilds. Sure, if you're accustomed to a fancy office and chauffeured car rides, crash-landing on an island would take a little adjustment.

But that doesn't mean a person is helpless. It might take a while to work up the nerve to pick snakes off you, but if you had to do it to survive you could if you were a strong person. That's the thing. A person's strength isn't always obvious right away..."

Without pausing in her chatter, she went to the refrigerator and retrieved more ingredients. When she came back and started slicing portobello mushrooms, Elam watched her lips move as she talked. And talked. And talked. He doubted he'd ever met a woman who talked as much as this one.

"Did you see that movie?"

He lifted his eyes. "What movie?"

"*The Horse Whisperer.* Haven't you been listening?"

"No."

She fell silent and stared at him.

"No, I didn't see that movie."

"Don't you ever watch movies?"

"I normally don't have time."

"Why not?"

"Because I work a lot."

She put the mushrooms in the frying pan along with some olive oil. "Killing people?" She glanced at him.

"Only the ones who deserve it," he said.

She stopped in the middle of picking up an onion. "What are you? Some kind of bounty hunter?"

"No."

"What then? An assassin?"

"I was a sniper in the army."

"You were a sniper?"

"Yes."

"Are you still?"

He didn't want to answer that. It would only lead to questions he couldn't answer. He watched her interpret his silence, and wariness mixed with curiosity in her eyes. Yes, he was still a sniper. He killed terrorists for a living and he didn't mind it at all.

"Are you still in the Army?" she asked.

She wanted him to assure her he at least operated within the law.

"No," he said. No one who worked for TES operated within the law. They'd never get anything accomplished if they did.

"Who do you work for now?"

There it was, the question he couldn't answer. TES operated under the guise of an infrastructure security consulting company, but how could he explain why he'd come to Bodrum to kill a man? "I'm a consultant."

"A consultant."

He smiled at the derision in her tone. She might be a blond beauty with a great rack, but she wasn't stupid. He took the onion from her. "I'll cut this for you."

"Who was that man you killed?" she asked.

"A bad guy."

"Why won't you tell me who he is?"

"Why won't you tell me why he boarded this yacht?" he countered.

Her beautiful amber eyes searched his. Did she know how transparent she was? She didn't trust him, but he sensed her hesitance didn't stem from anything depraved. She wore the body language of a victim. Why had someone like Ameen come after her? And had Elam solved her trouble by killing him or not?

Chapter 3

After dinner, Farren started Avril Lavigne's newest CD again. The cheerful and upbeat rhythm relaxed her. She was afloat with a man who killed people as a form of employment, one who didn't believe her when she said she knew nothing about why her attacker had singled her out. She couldn't explain why she didn't trust him. Maybe it was his deadly profession. What she knew of it. He obviously wasn't talking much about it, and his secretiveness made her uneasy.

She was afraid of what would happen to her after her attacker was discovered dead. Would the man who threatened her send someone else? Maybe she'd have enough time to go to Marmaris. She hoped so.

Farren sighed and sat on the floor. The Marmaris Yacht Festival started tomorrow. If she was stranded much longer, she might never know who owned the yacht called *Lucky*.

Putting her feet on a towel, she twisted the cap off a bottle of berry-colored nail polish.

As soon as they reached shore, she'd part ways with Elam and charter another yacht. He was suspicious of her, but her attacker was dead, so what reason would he have to stick around? He didn't strike her as the heroic type. He'd accomplished what he'd come to do and would be on his way. Then again, she didn't know anything about him. Her attacker had been a bad guy. What if Elam's methodical way of killing was clouding her judgment and he actually *was* the heroic type? His hardened self-assurance could be hiding a warm heart.

Her cold and loveless youth made it easy to recognize people like that, the ones who never let anyone in. Her heart was buried. Better that than suffer the consequences of exposing too much, feeling too much. Every time she'd done it as a child, allowed herself to show love, she'd been brushed off like an unwanted old dog. That kind of conditioning was hard to overcome as an adult. No wonder she was always settling for men who didn't love her. It was familiar.

Had Elam endured a similar past? Is that what drove him into such a deadly profession?

Hearing a hissed curse between songs, she looked toward the salon door. The sound came from above, on the flybridge. She put her nail polish aside and fanned her toes one last time before standing. Still holding the metal nail file, she hummed along with the song that was playing on her way up to the flybridge.

Elam sat with his legs spread, the bashed radio before him on the floor. He'd removed it from the console and taken the cover off to expose the inner electronics.

"Oh. Good thinking," she said, wishing she'd have thought of it herself.

He looked up.

"Are the parts still intact?" she asked.

"Aren't you sick of that music yet?" he all but snapped.

She smiled, knowing his annoyance came from the smashed radio and not her music, at least not this time. "You don't listen to music, either?"

"I listen to music, just not the same thing over and over again."

"I just got the CD before I came on this trip."

"And that's why you play the same music all the time?"

"If it's good. I like to listen to good music."

His intense blue eyes dropped to her Nautica swimsuit top. She'd changed and planned to sit in the hot tub after her nail polish dried. She tensed while his look heated up and lingered on her breasts cupped in lime-green nylon and spandex. His gaze dropped to her abdomen and her insides fluttered in response. She watched his eyes trail down the lime-green sarong tied around her waist, take in the length of leg peeking through the opening, then slowly come up again.

Ignoring the blatant inspection, she turned and started searching the broken instrument panel for a loose wire. She found a tin-plated copper wire from the tangle of a smashed gauge and sat cross-legged on the floor. Leaning forward, she used the nail file to scratch some conformal coat off the circuit board near the tuning knob. It hadn't been bashed all that bad. The channel knob and display were destroyed, but the guts of the radio were still intact.

Setting aside the file, she put one end of the wire to the metal she'd exposed and gently tapped the other end against another wire coming from the inner part of the channel knob. The radio crackled, but no one was talking on the channel she'd found.

Elam put his hand over hers, stopping her. She looked

up, startled by the jolt of awareness caused by his touch. Blue eyes held her riveted. She wanted to run her fingers through his dark chocolate hair, feel the warmth of his scalp. Feel those sensual lips on hers.

"I'll take it from here."

She let him have the wire, flustered by her reaction to such a man. It must have dawned on him that he could change channels by tapping the channel knob wire. He'd have to work at finding a channel of his choice without a display, but eventually he'd find one.

"Where did you learn how to do that?" he asked, holding the wire but not moving to try the channels.

"I have a masters in electrical engineering."

He looked surprised. "You're an engineer?"

It always irritated her when people were surprised that she had an engineering degree. "What's the matter? Don't I look like one?"

He made a show of taking in her chest and the leg that peeked through the opening of her sarong. Then he shook his head.

Why did men have to take her C-cup boobs and blond hair as signs of stupidity? It didn't help that she felt that way anyway, at least when it came to men. "You really *should* try to open your mind a little."

He chuckled. "That's not the problem."

"What is it then?"

He refrained from replying. Smart man. Instead, he ran his gaze fore and aft over the hundred-foot yacht.

"You must have a really good job to be able to afford to charter something like this," he said. "What are you? CEO of some Fortune 500 company?"

Reminded of her inheritance, her mood sank lower. "No."

"Entrepreneur?"

"No."

"Daddy set up a trust fund?"

She shook her head.

"What'd you do, embezzle it?" He chuckled. "Someone like you could probably get away with it. One look and nobody'd guess you were capable." He paused. "Not that... It's just that..."

His fumbling saved him a defensive retort. "My mother left me the money."

"You inherited it?"

"I didn't even know where she lived until her lawyer called me." The animosity came out in her voice.

He didn't say anything, but he was no longer smiling.

"She probably felt guilty for abandoning me so she could marry a wealthy man who didn't like kids," she went on, giving vent to the hurt inside her. "He was twenty years older than her. She never contacted me. I was only four when she left me in front of the emergency room of a hospital. I don't remember much about her. Mostly I just remember the day she left me. She was wearing a yellow sundress and she was crying. I wanted to make her stop. I thought I did something wrong. The police never found her. I became a ward of the state and was put in a foster home."

"How did she die?" he asked softly.

"Her husband shot her. But she got a shot off herself before she died and ended up killing him, too."

"Not a happy marriage, I take it."

She nodded and wondered what he'd do if she told him she thought it was more than that. Help her? It was tempting to tell him. He was obviously capable. But she was only here for answers. Once she went to the yacht festival, found the *Lucky* and got answers from whoever was on it, she'd go home. She could finish working through the emotions that had sprung to life after inheriting a fortune from a mother who hadn't cared what happened to her as a child. Talking about it had put an ache in her chest.

"Let me know when you reach someone who can come and get us." Pushing herself to her feet, she headed for the stairs, thoughts of her mother hanging in her mind like low fog.

She made her way to the main deck and walked to the stern. Stopping near the rail, she folded her arms and stared at the sea.

"Farren."

She turned with the sound of Elam's voice.

"I'm sorry about your mother."

Warmth spread through her, unexpected and coming at her in a strong wave. She hoped he couldn't tell.

The next morning Farren woke to the yacht's gentle rocking. It was quiet. Shoving the covers aside, she climbed out of bed. The sheer material of her light pink nightgown floated around her thighs. Slipping into a robe, she left the master suite and entered the dining area. Coffee would be delightful.

Light brightened the sitting room from the sliding glass door that led to the aft deck. She stepped into the open room. On the coffee table lay Elam's gun and holster. A slight shift of her gaze made her stop.

Stretched out on the long, curving couch was Elam. He wore only jeans and the top two buttons were unfastened. The blanket that once had covered him was on the floor. So was a pillow. He lay with one muscled arm bent above his head. His other arm draped over his bare and broad chest. She drank in the sight of him. His stomach and waist rippled with sinewy muscle. A soft protrusion mounded his jeans, the open buttons giving her a glimpse of his underwear. The jeans didn't hide the strength of his thighs. She tried to avoid looking at the open buttons again, but awe drew her back there. A deep, warm response stirred in her.

Sensing his awareness, she moved her eyes. His looked back at her, the radiant blue of them glowing in patient but heated question. A tiny gasp accompanied her alarm.

She spun around and walked quickly into the galley. What was he doing sleeping in there? It wasn't as if there was a shortage of beds aboard this yacht. There were other cabins on the lower deck.

In the galley, she banged through cupboards and drawers until she had everything she needed to make coffee. Her hand jerked when she heard Elam enter the galley. His presence generated sexual energy. She felt naked underneath her robe. The halter-style nightgown gathered into delicate pleats where it held her breasts, but was sheer all the way to her thighs. She shut off the water and kept her back to him as she finished preparing the coffeemaker.

"I couldn't reach Osman last night."

She glanced over her shoulder. "Who's Osman?"

"Someone I know. He'll come and get us. I'll try again this morning."

"Okay." She retrieved two coffee mugs from a cabinet and set them on the counter, still keeping her back to him.

"I should have told you I was going to sleep on the couch," he said.

She looked at him over her shoulder, catching him checking out her butt in the robe. When his hungry eyes met hers, her heart tripped into a hotter beat. He'd buttoned his jeans but his chest was still bare. She wondered how it would feel to put her hands on him.

"Why did you?" she asked.

"I didn't want to be too far away from you."

She wanted to fan her face.

"In case something happened," he added.

"You don't have to worry about me," she said.

"I'm not worried."

She looked past him into the salon and saw the coffee table where his gun lay and understood why he wasn't. Then she turned her attention back to the coffeemaker and waited for it to finish brewing. She listened to Elam move around in the salon. She glanced at him once and saw him putting on his holster. He wore it against his bare skin. Rather than put on his shirt, he slipped the weapon into the holder and headed toward her.

When the coffee was done, she poured him a cup. He took it from her with a murmured thanks, looking at her over the rim of the cup as he sipped.

Feeling a notable response to his interest, she took her cup and hurried to her cabin.

After a long shower she changed into a navy-blue Leilani swimsuit with big, overlapping white circles. She couldn't push the memory of Elam's eyes from her mind. It was definitely good that they would part ways. He'd devour her and she'd be left with another desperate reach for affection.

She clasped the back of her suit. It had a gold ring at the center of the bandeau top and a neck tie for support. She wrapped a matching sarong around her waist and headed outside with a book and a tube of sunscreen, propping a pair of sunglasses on top of her head. Maybe reading in the sun would take her mind off what was going on. Climbing the stairs to the sundeck, she spotted Elam in the flybridge, holding the binoculars to his eyes, chest still bare except for the gun and holster.

She hesitated, uncertain how much more of his nearness she could handle.

He lowered the binoculars and saw her. "Did you get a hold of Osman?" she asked.

He nodded. "I'm not sure how far we've drifted, but he should find us before too long."

Pulling her sunglasses over her eyes, she passed him, feeling him watch her as she put her book and sunscreen down and removed her sarong. After draping the sarong over the back of the bench seat that divided the sunbathing pad from the flybridge, she applied sunscreen and then reclined on the pad, her back against the bench seat. Telling herself there was no reason to be nervous, she put on her sunglasses, opened her book and started to read. That lasted all of thirty seconds.

Elam climbed onto the sunbathing pad and reclined next to her. She looked over at him. He wore sunglasses so she couldn't see his eyes, but his mouth was curved into a licentious grin.

"What are you doing?" she asked.

"Catching some sun."

"Mmm-hmm."

He just kept grinning. "What are you reading?"

She showed him the cover.

"The Good Girl's Guide to Bad Men?" he read.

"I caught my fiancé sleeping with someone else."

"And you think that book is going to help you avoid men like that?"

"I'll try anything once."

"Why don't you just live alone for a while? Maybe you're trying too hard."

His insight surprised her. She eyed him from behind the security of her sunglasses, taking in his bare chest and gun. "Does that work for you?"

"I've never had a woman cheat on me."

"Have you ever had one long enough to give her the chance?"

He turned away, looking out to sea.

"You have." And from the looks of him, it hadn't gone well. "Were you married? Are you still?"

"No."

"You were married to her?" she asked.

"Yes."

"What happened?" She knew it might be too personal, but she couldn't stop herself from asking.

"I should have known from the beginning that it would never work."

"But you wanted it to."

"I wouldn't have married her if I didn't."

She believed him. He didn't strike her as a man who didn't know what he wanted.

"She must have been interesting," she said out loud.

But she could see he was finished talking about her.

Farren was strangely touched by the idea of him loving someone. Or was it the realization that he was capable of that?

She looked at his sunglasses, wishing she could see his eyes. "What would you do if she came back to you?"

His jaw flexed with tension. "She wouldn't."

"But what if she did?"

"She won't."

"But—"

The sound of a boat approaching interrupted their conversation. She turned to look out to sea, where the white shape of a boat broke the water.

"Is that Osman?"

"Yes, that's his fishing vessel."

She shifted her gaze from the fifty-foot boat with

enclosed pilothouse to Elam. So this was it. Pretty soon she'd never see him again.

As he pulled himself up from the sunbathing pad, his stomach muscles flexed and distracted her. He crawled over her, straddling her as he moved to stand. All that masculinity engulfed her.

He extended his hand. She took it and he helped her to her feet. She sucked in a breath of air as he put his hands on her waist and she had nowhere else to put hers but on his chest.

"You should go change," he said.

She felt the heat growing between them despite what his sunglasses hid. A few more days with him and where would she be? On her back for sure, but after the days passed? Right smack in the middle of another mistake, that was where.

After docking at Bodrum Marina, Elam pulled Farren's luggage toward a waiting car. He got in beside her after handing the luggage to the driver. She looked at him in the same way she'd been doing ever since he'd told her about his wife. Curious and somewhat bewildered.

As much as he wanted to immerse himself in her flowery sweetness, there was no point in starting anything. A night or two wouldn't be enough for a woman like her, and he couldn't give her more. He'd just make sure she made it to a hotel before he found a room somewhere else. He wanted to check her out a little more, get some background on her, just to make sure he hadn't missed anything, and there was a reason Ameen had chosen her yacht.

When the car stopped in front of the Hotel Karia Princess, Elam climbed out and helped the driver pull Farren's luggage from the trunk. He rolled it toward her, noticing how she glanced around, as though looking for something or someone. Was she worried? But then she turned to him, and as she watched him come to a stop, a sultry awareness came into her eyes.

"Thank you," she said. She rocked onto her toes and back down. Was he making her nervous? "It seems like it's been more than a day since you came aboard *Haven.*" She smiled a little. "This reminds me of a movie I saw once. It was an action film that took place over twenty-four hours. So much was going on in such a short period of time…" And on she went.

He was starting to think all that sweet chatter was a nervous reaction. Instead of listening, he used the opportunity to burn her into his memory. The white halter sundress with a slight flare at her knees. The necklace with a clear stone and the word *Sun* embedded inside. The light cinnamon-colored gloss on her lips. Femininity radiated from her. He wanted to drown himself in it. Or at least take some home with him.

"It's amazing how much you can get done in not so much time. That happens when I go shopping, too," he heard her say. Yeah, he was going to have to take some of this home with him. "The time just flies b—"

He took a step closer, watching her eyes widen when she realized what he was doing. Sliding his hand to the small of her back, he pulled her against him. The sound of her breath whooshing out of her sent something dark and intimate rushing through him. Bending his head, he kissed her gently. Because that was the only way to kiss a woman like her the first time.

Her soft body melted against him, a perfect fit against his. Her hands ran up his chest, catching on the straps of his gun holster. He felt her thumbs glide over his nipples as she opened her mouth against his, asking for more. He gave it to her, kissing her with painstaking gentleness.

Slow and sensual. Her fingers brushed the ends of his hair at his collar as she languidly folded her arms around him. God Almighty, she felt good. Bringing his other hand to her back, he held her tighter to him as he reached deeper with his tongue for a soft, sweet taste. Fire roared inside him. If he didn't stop now, he just might go with her to her room. Reining in the powerful surge of desire swimming in him, he lifted his head.

Traffic passed behind him and people walked by. The sound of her catching her breath, the look of passion in her amber eyes, her moist lips. It all wrapped around him. He wanted to bury himself in her femininity. Have it surround him while he made love to her.

She smiled, her lips inching up knowingly, sweetly, a secret she shared with him, this intimacy.

He let her go. Nothing could have prepared him for the way it felt to kiss her. He knew it would be good, but…damn!

She took the handle of her luggage and walked toward the hotel, her gait carefree. Halfway to the door, she looked back, still smiling. He almost started to go after her. A will of iron kept his feet from moving.

Then he noticed a figure leaning against the concrete wall beside the front entrance of the hotel. Farren turned forward and he saw the man watch her enter the hotel. Not a tall man, he was dark-haired and wore tan trousers with a short-sleeved, collared blue shirt. Pretending not to notice, Elam turned and got back into the car.

The man looked from the car to Farren.

"Pull out into the street and park just past the hotel," Elam told the driver.

The driver complied. Elam saw the man outside the hotel push off the wall and follow Farren inside.

What was this all about?

Elam paid the driver and climbed out, jogging to the hotel entrance. Inside, he spotted Farren checking in at the counter and the dark-haired man holding a newspaper thirty feet away. Elam stopped near a plant. The man hadn't noticed him. He was too busy watching Farren over the top edge of the newspaper.

What the hell?

Elam undid one of his shirt buttons and flipped the safety off his silenced pistol. He heard a bellman say he'd bring Farren's luggage to her room in a few minutes. When she started toward the stairs, the dark-haired man followed.

A familiar adrenaline rush triggered his pulse into readiness. He strode purposefully toward the dark-haired man's back. Farren turned to look toward the front door of the hotel, as if hoping to catch one last glimpse of him. An impish smile softened her profile. He was glad she was still distracted by that kiss. He needed her to keep walking, to get them away from so many people.

She began to climb the curving white marble stairs. The man followed but kept glancing around. A couple coming down the stairs passed her and the man.

Elam climbed the stairs behind a tall, fat man, staying out of sight in case either she or the man following her turned. On the second level, the fat man went a different way than Farren. She made her way down a hall.

Slipping his hand inside his shirt, Elam gripped his gun. She stopped at a room door.

The man who'd followed her turned to look behind him. Elam pulled his gun from its holster. Farren saw him and her mouth fell open. Her gaze went to his gun, then flashed to the man, who bolted into a run down the hall.

"Go into your room and wait for me," Elam growled as he went after the man.

He chased him to the ground level and out a back door. The man sprinted down an alley. Elam let him go. He didn't want to leave Farren alone.

He went back into the hotel and jogged up the stairs. Making his way to Farren's room door, he knocked. "It's me. Open the door."

She did, looking pale as she backed into the room to give him space to enter.

He shut the door. "Who was that?"

She shook her head.

"You don't know?"

"How would I? I've never been here before."

He angled his head as he studied her. She knew something and had kept it from him. Her eyes grew wary as he stepped closer.

"Why did he come after you?"

Her eyes blinked, revealing her uncertainty.

"Why did Ameen Al-Jabbar board your yacht?" he demanded.

The way she stared at him he couldn't tell if she knew the name. She turned and wandered to the balcony door, where she stopped and crossed her arms. He followed, stopping behind her, trying not to be affected by the slope of her neck and the bare skin her halter dress exposed.

He put his hand on her upper arm and guided her to face him. Her gaze searched his.

"I know you were the reason he boarded your yacht," he said. "And now another man came after you. Tell me why."

Still, she hesitated. "I shouldn't have come here."

He took in her slender form in a pretty white dress, the pink fingernail polish and the smooth skin of her delicate hands resting on slim biceps.

"I couldn't agree more," he said.

"I know I wasn't followed to the airport. I made sure of it. How would anyone have known I was in Bodrum?"

"Why did you think you'd be followed?"

She let out a tight breath. "A man threatened to kill me if I didn't pay him three million dollars. He claimed my mother's husband owed it to him, but he refused to say why. He knows where I live. He delivered a bloody scarf of my neighbor's to my door. It scared me. He was serious."

"Yeah. I'd say three million makes it pretty serious." He took in her worried frown. "So you come to Turkey to what? Chase him down?" He tried to keep the sarcasm out of his voice but couldn't.

"Ameen must have worked for him."

"Ameen is working for someone?" His mind began to race.

"The caller was in the United States and knew a lot about me. How close I am to my neighbor. Where I live…"

Elam barely paid attention. The idea of Ameen answering to someone meant the terror cell was more complicated than his current intelligence revealed. Osman hadn't dug deep enough. This was mushrooming into something bigger than Cullen had known.

"Why did you come to Bodrum, Farren?"

Now her eyes focused on him. "I didn't know what else to do. I can't just hand over that kind of money to a stranger. And I was afraid to go to the police. The caller warned me not to. What if the police couldn't do anything to help me?"

"Why did you come to Turkey? Why Bodrum?"

"My mother chartered a yacht here. I wanted to know why. I think she was going to meet someone in Marmaris."

"Marmaris."

"There's a yacht festival there."

Had Ameen planned to go there as well? Elam had seen him go into a yacht charter office the day before he'd followed him to Farren. He'd wondered why but hadn't thought any more on it. "What can you tell me about your mother's husband?"

"He was wealthy and hated children."

"What did he do for a living?"

"He owned a shipping business. I don't remember the name of it."

That could be important. He tucked the information away for now.

"I don't know very much about him," Farren added.

He believed her. "Ameen is a terrorist, Farren," he said and watched her eyes widen.

"What?"

"Whatever business your stepfather was involved in, it may have been with terrorists."

She looked across the room, dazed and frightened. Abruptly, she went to her purse and dug out her cell phone. "I have to get out of here." She sounded breathless. "I should have never come in the first place. Terrorists. My God. If I'd known that I never would have flown here."

"It doesn't matter where you go now. They'll find you. It's clear enough that whoever threatened you will go to any length to get you. And your coming here only shows him you aren't going to give him the money."

"That's right. I'm going home and I'm calling the police."

He grunted. Did she actually think that would do any good? "You'll be lucky to make it to the airport, sweetheart."

She froze in the act of pressing a number. Then fiery amber eyes rolled to glare at him. "Don't call me that."

He sighed. He hadn't meant to. It was just her effect on

him. Her femininity made him too protective. "You can't go home. It's too late for that."

She stared at him in disbelief.

"What makes you think your mother planned to meet someone at the yacht festival?"

She plopped her butt onto the bed, looking down at the cell phone still in her hands. He listened as she explained about the notes her mother wrote. "I thought it was strange she chartered a yacht in Bodrum and was going to go to the festival all by herself."

"How did you know it was related to the threats?"

"I didn't."

"You didn't." Why the hell had she risked coming here then?

"I didn't know what else to do."

"You're lucky you ran into me."

She eyed him reproachfully. "You're awfully sure of yourself."

"If you hadn't, you'd have been kidnapped and by now forced to…what?"

"Wire transfer the money to a numbered account. He gave me wire instructions." Resignation seeped into her tone.

"And once you performed it, whoever's behind this would have killed you." He paused to make sure she heard what he said next. "After having some fun with you first. There's nothing a terrorist loves more than an opportunity to torture an American woman."

She seemed numb now, but at least he got his point through. He didn't want her going off on her own. She needed him whether she liked it or not.

"What are we going to do now?" she asked.

"We need information. First we'll go to Osman. It was his contact that led me to Ameen. I need a name."

Chapter 4

"I can't remember the name of the movie, but that scene was so fake." The taxi jostled Farren as she talked. Elam looked at her. He hadn't stopped looking at her since they'd left the hotel. "I mean, the hospital was empty. How many hospitals have you been to that were empty? Sure, it was late at night, but come on, people don't get sick or hurt on schedule." She didn't know what made her think of this particular horror movie. Maybe it was seeing Elam coming down the hotel hall with his gun drawn. "And why did the villain go into an operating room and start whacking people? It didn't make any sense. What motive did he have for doing it? Going into a hospital and killing anyone and everyone. It was done just for horror appeal, you know?"

He just kept staring at her. She hadn't stopped talking since they'd left the hotel. She couldn't help it. She was still punchy from seeing Elam chase a man who'd obviously followed her and would have done God-only-knew-what to her. And, of course, there was that kiss.

Farren was far too aware of Elam sitting next to her in the backseat of the taxi, oozing sex appeal. His shirt was still partially unbuttoned, making for easy access to his gun. Knees parted, he appeared as relaxed as could be, but she knew better. He was ready for anything.

The taxi stopped and she finally had to look away. Elam said something to the driver as he paid for the fare. Climbing out of the taxi with him, she walked beside him toward a white mortar villa in the hills north of the marina. He put his hand on her lower back as they approached the front door. She almost flinched with the touch.

She wasn't supposed to see him again. That farewell kiss was just supposed to be a nice memory. Now here they were, together. What if he kissed her again? Would it lead to more? How long was she going to have to be with him?

He rang the doorbell and searched their surroundings, making it seem that his hand on her back was out of protectiveness rather than intimacy. She ought to be glad. She didn't know him very well, but she doubted a sniper was the man of her dreams.

Osman opened the door with a questioning frown. Elam told him what happened at the hotel as they entered the villa. The interior was open and surprisingly modern. Farren didn't know what she expected a home in Turkey to look like, but it wasn't this. A spacious sitting area with wicker furniture and a red mosaic rug blended with a dining table and kitchen that had up-to-date appliances and tile flooring.

"Who could have followed you to the hotel?" Osman asked when Elam finished talking.

"That's why we're here."

A woman emerged from a stairway. She had graying hair and dark eyes and wore a long-sleeved blouse with tan slacks.

"Elam," the woman greeted him.

"Hello, Meryem." He gestured to Farren. "This is Farren Gage."

"Ah, yes, Osman told me about your rescue. How frightening it must have been to be stranded at sea!" Meryem walked over to Farren and took her hand in a brief grasp. "But you couldn't have been in more capable hands. Welcome."

"Thank you," Farren said, smiling.

"Come, I will take you to the terrace," Osman said. "It is a fine day. We will talk there."

"I'll bring some apple tea," Meryem said, going into the kitchen.

Elam touched Farren's back again, guiding her to walk ahead of him and behind Osman as they climbed the stairs. On the rooftop terrace, she was momentarily swept away by the view. She went to stand near a Turkish corner bench with red and blue and yellow pillows. Rolling mandarin groves stretched down the hill. The town center and the marina were in the distance. Red shingled rooftops dotted the landscape and the Castle of St. Peter was visible.

Osman sat with Elam on the bench. "What brings you to see me?" he asked. "I am sorry to hear someone is after Ms. Gage, but how is this related to me or any information I have given you?"

"I need the name of your contact, Osman. The one who told you about Ameen."

Osman's expression grew guarded. "I do not reveal the identities of my contacts. You know this."

"I'm asking you to make an exception."

"I do not understand. Are you afraid whoever followed you and Farren to the hotel is linked to Ameen? How?"

"Ameen was working with someone else. Someone I'm afraid has more dangerous connections and may be planning something in Marmaris."

"How do you know this?" Elam glanced at Farren, and she knew he'd drawn this conclusion because of what she'd told him about her mother. Terrorists had threatened her for money…but why did he think they'd planned something in Marmaris?

"I saw Ameen go into a yacht charter company before he went after Farren."

"And did he charter a yacht to Marmaris?"

"I don't know, but I will after I go to the charter company."

Did the terrorists know her mother was going to go there and meet someone? Was it that someone the terrorists were after? Then why not just go there and kill the person? Why follow her mother's itinerary? Or was it the other way around…had her mother known about the terrorists' itinerary?

"Do you think Ameen was trying to stop me from going to Marmaris?" she asked Elam.

He turned to her. "It's possible."

"How did they know we'd come back to the marina after you killed Ameen?" Ameen's body probably wouldn't turn up for days.

"They might not have been sure. When Ameen didn't show up wherever he was supposed to take you, someone must have sent another man to watch the marina. There was time, since we were stranded at sea for a while."

As she thought about that, Elam faced their host.

"I need to talk to your contact, Osman."

Worry put a line above his nose. "If my contact knew more, he would have told me. He would not have kept anything from me."

"Whoever Ameen was working with wants money from Farren and doesn't want anyone knowing why. If your contact learned more about Ameen after he delivered his initial information and Ameen's friends found out…"

Farren watched Osman begin to waver.

"Please, Osman. You could save his life if you tell me who he is and where I can find him."

"You truly think his life is in danger?"

"Yes."

"Then I will go to him myself. If he knows more of Ameen's affairs, I will pass the information along as I have always done."

"No. I don't want you involved anymore. This is getting too dangerous. Tell me his name and where I can find him. I'll make sure he's all right."

Osman took several moments before he finally replied. "Asil is his name." He told Elam where to find him in Bodrum.

Meryem appeared on the terrace, smiling as she carried four cups of tea on a tray. She put the tray on the low table before the bench seat and brought a cup over to Farren.

Farren took it. "Thank you." She looked over at Elam, wondering what they'd uncover when they found Osman's contact. She wasn't sure she wanted to go with him, but, of course, he wouldn't have it any other way now. What if Asil was already dead?

"Sometimes I wish my Osman would stop his cavorting with Elam and that company he works for," Meryem surprised her by saying.

Farren looked at her. "He and Osman work together?"

"When the occasion warrants it." Meryem's tone and eyes said she didn't like it.

"How long have they known each other?"

"Just two years. When Elam came to work for Cullen."

"Cullen?"

"That is who pays my Osman for his work. He is not a direct employee like Elam, but the money comes from the same place."

"What's the name of the company that employs them?"

"As I have said, Osman does not work directly for the company. TES, he calls it, but what it does, what its purpose is, I do not know. I am not sure I want to know. Osman cannot talk of the things he does, but I know he would never do anything immoral. He is working for the good of this world. That is enough for me."

What kind of company hired snipers? One that fought terrorism? She resisted the appeal of that. Elam had told her he was a consultant after admitting he was a sniper. "Doesn't it bother you that he keeps secrets?"

"I do not see them as secrets. It is more important to me that Osman is happy. And I see that he is."

Farren wasn't sure she could be so forgiving. "It must take a special kind of person to do what your husband does."

"My husband works in the background. His life is rarely in danger. Elam…well, his life is always in danger."

Farren looked over at him. He still spoke with Osman. "Why does he do it?"

"Elam? Why does any man put himself in dangerous situations on foreign land? For God and country? Honor? Duty? Yes, I believe all that. But Osman says Elam has a troubled past and that is what drives him."

Was this what lurked beneath Elam's hardened shell? Farren tried not to get too caught up in her curiosity. "What kind of troubled past?"

"He was married once."

Well, lots of people married and lots of people divorced.

But she remembered Elam's reaction when they talked about his wife.

"Veronica left him in a way that scarred Elam," Meryem said.

Veronica. Somehow a name made her more real. And the knowledge that Elam had truly loved a woman reached past her defenses and stung her.

"What happened?" she asked.

"The day she left him, she was in a terrible car accident and was killed. It happened the same day she told him she wanted a divorce. Elam did not take it well. He loved her and she died before she could get away from him."

The unexpectedness of the revelation stopped Farren.

What would you do if she came back to you?

She wouldn't...

She wouldn't because she was dead.

Elam had just finished talking to Osman and stood. As he approached her, she could only stare at him while apprehension filled her. She'd spent her childhood accepting crumbs of affection. She didn't want to keep living like that. And if she wanted change, if she wanted a man who loved her more than any other woman, she had to stop turning to men who only had crumbs to offer.

"We need to go," he said, touching her lower back. She fought the warm tingle his hand gave her as he guided her toward the door.

After leaving Osman's house, they'd checked Farren out of the Karia Princess and taken a taxi to a car-rental place. Now they were at a hotel near the marina. Elam didn't want to stay at the Karia Princess, not since someone had seen them there. He rooted through his duffel bag for his cell phone. Farren stood over by the hotel-room door, uncharacteristically quiet. He had a headache from her talking the entire time they'd lined up a rental car and driven here, and now she wasn't talking. But he did have an idea what was making her so uncomfortable, and it was more than the threat for money.

"I want you in the same room with me," he said. "In case someone comes after you again."

She nodded, but wasn't any more relaxed.

At least she understood. What did she think he was going to do? Climb on top of her when the lights were off? He felt a smile inch up a corner of his mouth.

After finding his phone, he pulled a picture of Ameen out of a zippered compartment of the duffel and then stood. Stuffing the picture in his back pocket, he looked at Farren. She gripped her hands together and eyed him. Her dainty sandals flattered trim ankles and the white halter dress showcased her amazing breasts. How a woman like her got tangled up in a mess like this baffled him. All her soft curves made her a misfit for this situation. Either that or the perfect target.

"Let's go." He headed for the door and the parking lot.

On the way, he pressed Cullen's Roaring Creek, Colorado, number into the cell. With the phone to his ear, he opened the passenger door for Farren. She got in and closed the door.

"Yeah," Odie answered.

He climbed into the car. "Odie, it's Elam." A quick glance confirmed that Farren watched him.

"Hang on, let me conference Cullen in," Odie said. "He's been waiting to hear from you." Less than a minute later, Cullen was on the line.

"What happened?" Cullen demanded.

"I got the package."

"You didn't check in at the scheduled time." Cullen sounded angry.

"Something came up that I wasn't expecting." He glanced over at Farren, who sat in the passenger seat running pink-painted fingernails through silky blond hair and was still looking out the window. Her pretty white dress pooled around her thighs and knees. The *Sun* necklace nestled in her cleavage.

Unexpected to be sure. Ire tightened in his head, making it ache more. At least she wasn't talking his ears raw.

He told Cullen and Odie everything, including what happened after he'd kissed Farren goodbye in front of the Hotel Karia Princess. Well, almost everything. Elam left out the fact that he had, in fact, kissed her. And, oh, what a kiss.

"Ameen knew the Gage woman?" Odie sounded incredulous.

"Someone sent him."

"Wait a minute," Odie said. "Why was he in Bodrum? Was he casing his next target like we thought or did he know the Gage woman was going to be there?"

Elam had always thought Odie had a tough, brilliant mind. What he didn't get was why it didn't turn him on the way it used to. "He might not have known she was going to be there, but once she appeared, his plans changed."

"To kidnapping her?" Odie asked.

"Yes," Elam answered.

"Did Ameen know you were chasing him?" Cullen asked.

"No, but I lost him in the marina and only caught up to him when he got into a boat and then boarded Farren's yacht. I didn't think he saw me, but I wondered why he motored to that yacht. I should have known something was wrong right then."

"How could you have known he was planning to kidnap Farren?" Cullen said. "You didn't even know of her existence until you climbed aboard her chartered yacht."

"This could actually work in our favor," Odie said. "If Ameen didn't know you were following him, he probably assumed you were just trying to help Farren when you came after him."

"Right," Cullen said. "He'd have no other reason to think one American man, dressed like a tourist, would be after him. And neither would whoever he was working for. It's a great cover. You rescue a beautiful woman and hook up with her."

"You want me to play the part of her boyfriend?" It wouldn't take much effort.

He sensed Farren stir beside him.

"Okay, let's go over what Ameen's boss knows," Odie said. "He sends Ameen after Farren, but the attempt fails. Someone is sent to watch the marina when Ameen doesn't show up wherever he planned to take Farren. You and Farren show up, and the guy follows you to the Hotel Karia Princess, where he sees you say goodbye to your new sweetheart."

"Sounds good so far," Elam said.

"Did you make it look good?"

"Make what look good?"

"The goodbye. Was it obvious you were hot for her?"

Elam didn't say anything. He couldn't. Odie was far too good at reading between the lines.

"You kissed her, didn't you?"

"That hardly matters."

"It matters a great deal. It'll dictate how we play this from here on out."

"Odie's right," Cullen interjected. "Just tell us if you think it looked convincing. I don't need to hear the details…unlike Odie, who gets off on that sort of thing."

"Hey, I only seek the truth."

Elam looked at Farren, who'd stopped feigning she wasn't listening and now focused on his conversation. Her big amber eyes were as innocent as they were intelligent. He wanted to do more than kiss her.

"Yeah, it was pretty convincing."

Odie laughed. "Perfect."

"What's the mother's name?" Cullen asked. "Odie, I want you to find everything you can on her and the husband."

"No problem."

Elam moved the phone away from his mouth and asked Farren, "What was your mother's name?"

"Carolyn Fenning."

"Carolyn Fenning," Elam said into the phone.

"I'll get everything I can find on the daughter, too," Odie said.

"Just Carolyn and her husband, Jared," Elam disagreed, focusing on the road. "Don't waste time digging for anything on Farren."

Odie whistled into the phone. "Getting a little protective, are we?"

"Farren isn't working with Ameen's friends," Elam said. "She's on our side."

"Is she beautiful?" Odie asked.

"Odie, quit with the meddling," Cullen put in.

"I bet she is," Odie said anyway. "What did you say her full name was? Farren. Farren Gage."

Elam heard her typing the name on her keyboard. And everybody knew Odie had all the links she needed to get information on people.

"There she goes," Cullen quipped. "My sympathies, pal. I've been where you are before. She's merciless…"

"Thanks," Elam said dryly.

"That's not what I'm looking for," Odie mumbled, still clicking, ignoring both him and Cullen. "Oh, here we go. Oh, yeah. Lookie what we have here. Long blond hair. Brown eyes. Hmm. Never had you figured for one of those. She's a knockout, though. A little prissy for you, but very pretty."

Elam looked over at Farren, fresh as a sunny spring day, watching him.

"What's she do?" Odie asked. Elam heard her clicking away on her computer. "Oh, never mind. An electrical engineer, huh? Hmm, she doesn't look like one. I'd have pegged her for an underwear model or something."

Elam let out an involuntary laugh. He had to agree. He could see Farren as an underwear model, too. In fact, he'd like her to model some just for him.

"Jealous?" he said into the phone.

"You're not my type."

"All right, enough tormenting Elam," Cullen said. "Elam, I'm sending you a team. Tell Osman we'll need the airstrip in his friend's village."

"Will do. But I need one more thing."

"Shoot," Cullen said.

"A Delphie Sinclair is going to need some protection until this is all over." He explained who she was and gave them the sister's name after Farren told him what it was.

"Anything else?"

"Yeah. Tell the team they're going to pose as my crew. We're going to Marmaris."

"What's in Marmaris?"

"A yacht festival."

"Check back when you get there," Cullen said.

"Will do." He disconnected the call.

"Was that your boss?" Farren asked.

He didn't answer as he pulled up in front of Asil's apartment building. There were missing shingles on the roof and the building's pale yellow paint was chipping. Unkempt gardens more closely resembled weeds. A cracked and uneven sidewalk led to each weathered blue door.

Elam got out of the rental car and met Farren on the other side. He took her hand as they walked toward the building, not liking the neighborhood, or how dark it was getting. At the apartment door, he knocked.

No one answered.

He knocked again. Still, no answer. He glanced at Farren before trying the door handle. She looked around her, as though worried someone would catch them.

He gave her a reassuring smile.

"I'm not any good at this," she admitted. "This mystery-solving stuff, I mean. I read a few mystery novels now and then, but that's the extent of my exposure. I think the closest I've come to a dangerous situation was the time I blew a stop sign when I was sixteen. A van hit my left front fender. I bumped my head and—"

"It's okay," he cut her off before she kept going. "I won't let anything happen to you."

"What if something's happened to him?" She gestured toward the door with her eyes and head.

He didn't answer because he was afraid something already had. Letting go of her hand, he turned the knob. The door wasn't locked. Taking one more look around, he pulled his gun out of his holster and pushed open the door. The apartment was dark. He led Farren into the living room. There was a sagging couch on a faded and torn area rug and a small TV on a square stand in the corner.

He stopped at the threshold of a hall and thought twice before bringing her with him. "Wait here." He guided her so she leaned against the wall, out of view of any windows. Then he made his way down the hall, pointing his gun in the bathroom and first bedroom. When he came to the second bedroom, he lowered his weapon.

Asil lay on the bed, blood staining the sheet that partially covered him. He'd been shot in the chest. It looked like he hadn't died right away because he'd reached for the table beside the bed, and in his hand was a crumpled piece of paper. It also looked like he hadn't been killed all that long ago. Last night probably.

Elam pulled the paper out of his dead fingers. Opening it, he read a blurb about the yacht festival. He looked down at the body.

"I sure wish you could talk," he muttered. What was so important about this damn yacht festival?

A choked sound behind him made him look toward the door. Farren stood there with her hand over her mouth and eyes round with horror.

Elam folded the paper and shoved it in his back pocket where he'd also put a photograph of Ameen. "I told you to wait."

Going to her, he put his arm around her waist and led her back down the hall.

"I think I'm going to be sick." She covered her mouth with one hand and her stomach with the other.

She wasn't cut out for this. He took her back into the living room and sat her on the couch, waiting to make sure she didn't throw up.

"I need to look around," he said. "Are you all right?"

She nodded, taking a deep, steady breath.

He left her there and began to search the house. When nothing turned up, he returned to Farren. Her face still looked a little pale but she seemed more together now.

He held out his hand. "Let's go."

She took his hand and he led her outside. He opened the car door and she got in. After going around to the driver's side, he got in and sat behind the wheel.

"I should have just transferred the money like that man on the phone wanted," she said. "Then maybe that man inside wouldn't have been killed."

"It isn't your fault Asil was killed. He knew something Ameen's leader didn't want him to know. Asil didn't know about the money. If he had, Osman would have known and he would have told me. Things would have been different."

She still looked torn up about what happened and it gave his heart a twist.

"Asil knew what Ameen and his friends were planning in Marmaris. That's why he was killed," he said.

Her lower lip trembled and she put it in the clamp of her white, straight teeth. If she cried, he was going to have to pull over.

"But if I hadn't come to Bodrum, he wouldn't have been killed."

"You forget I came here to kill Ameen. They would have gone after Asil anyway. They wouldn't have wanted me talking to him."

"Do you think they knew he was talking to Osman?" she asked.

"No. I think he stumbled onto something and then couldn't get the information on Marmaris to Osman in time." The way he'd clutched the brochure suggested as much.

She didn't ask any more questions, so he called Osman to let him know what happened. He parked at the Marina Vista Hotel.

When Farren started walking toward the hotel entrance,

he put his arm around her and guided her the other way, toward the marina.

"Where are we going now?" she asked, sounding weary.

She wasn't used to people chasing her and seeing dead bodies. He understood that. But she was going to have to toughen up.

"To the yacht charter office Ameen went to."

"But Ameen is dead."

"His friends aren't." He took her hand, led her across a busy street, and they entered the marina.

After making their way through a parking area and past the Coast Guard building, Elam opened the door to the Williams Yacht Charter Company.

Inside, the woman behind the counter looked up and smiled. Elam greeted her in English, hoping she'd understand him. She answered in kind.

He pulled out the photograph from his back pocket and showed it to her. Her smile vanished.

"Do you recognize this man?" Elam asked.

The woman nodded. "He was rude man. Yes, I recognize. His name Ameen. Why are you looking for him? Is he in trouble with law?"

"Something like that. Did he charter a yacht?"

"Yes. It is still scheduled to depart." She typed on the computer keyboard. "Tomorrow. I give them *Sea Minstrel.* You here to arrest him, no?"

"Did he give you names of anyone sailing with him?" He didn't answer her question.

"We require on all charters. One moment." She went to find the paperwork on the charter. When she returned, she turned the page she found so Elam could read it. Farren leaned close and read the names.

They were all Arabic.

"Do you have a piece of paper?" Elam asked.

"I copy for you." She made the copy and handed it to him with a satisfied smile.

"Thank you." He folded the paper and tucked it away with the photograph. "Now, I'd like to charter a yacht myself. What have you got available for the same dates our friend Ameen booked?"

The woman's smile expanded. "We have many nice yachts. I show you and give you good deal."

"I need a shower," Farren complained as they walked toward the marina entrance on their way back to the hotel near the marina. She was bone tired. Didn't this guy ever rest? Would this day ever end? It was hard for her to believe it had been only this morning that Osman had rescued them.

"After we eat," Elam said.

Come to think of it, she hadn't eaten since this morning.

"Can't I shower first? And change? I feel grimy." Had it only been this morning that she'd last showered? It seemed like days ago.

"You look great. Let's eat first." He put his hand on her lower back and steered her to the right before reaching the marina entrance.

Typical man. He said "you look great" as if he were trained to.

"Is it safe? Can't we order room service?"

"It's safe."

She looked at his profile and then her gaze ran down to his chest, remembering the gun hidden under his shirt.

"Of course. How could I forget?" she quipped.

At the Marina Yacht Club, they were seated outside on a balcony that overlooked another area of tables. People gathered at a square bar and milled around tables. Chatter blended with the light sound of a band playing on a covered stage. There was a clear view of docked boats, masts of sailboats spearing the night sky.

A waiter appeared and Elam ordered wine. When the waiter left, he lifted the dinner menu.

"I'll have whatever you're having," she said.

The waiter returned with a bottle of wine and Elam ordered the swordfish. When he left, Elam poured red wine into Farren's glass, filling it almost to the rim.

She smiled. "How did you know what I needed?" She lifted the glass and drank.

"You've had a rough day."

She leaned back, taking the glass with her, feeling her muscles relax. It was a warm evening for the middle of May. She took in the lights from all the boats and the Castle of St. Peter across the bay. The city of Bodrum sprawled along the shoreline.

She sipped more wine. Over the rim of her glass, she saw Elam leaning back in his chair with his chin on curled fingers, watching her with distinct male interest. He didn't seem to care that she'd caught him. He'd been looking at her like that a lot today. Maybe she'd have to watch the kind of clothes she wore around him.

"When I was thirteen, I started daydreaming about being rich and traveling the world," she said. He blinked slowly, the only sign that he knew she was about to start talking again. It was his fault. He made her nervous when he looked at her like that. She sipped her wine and continued. "I had servants and everywhere I went people adored me. I attended extravagant parties, had boys pining for my attention. I was smart. I even went yachting in one daydream. My foster parents' son teased me relentlessly when he found a yachting magazine I bought with my allowance money. He used to say nobody would ever want me. That I was too stupid and ugly and why didn't I just leave and make the rest of his family happy."

Farren couldn't tell if he was annoyed or listening. He just sat there all relaxed, watching her.

"Funny, now that I'm a millionaire, I don't want any of those things. I just want people to appreciate me for who I am. I like my simple life in Bar Harbor. I don't want mansions and servants and fancy cars. Yachting is nice, but I don't need it."

"Did you know you talk a lot when you're nervous?" he asked.

And she melted. She was nervous. He was right. She was nervous because he'd kissed her earlier in the day and she was anticipating him doing it again.

"Nothing will happen you don't want."

Nothing she didn't want. A flutter settled low in her abdomen. That's what scared her. She was afraid she wanted too much.

"Have you always lived in Bar Harbor?" he asked when she said nothing more.

Was it the wine that was starting to make her feel hot or him? "Um…I—I moved there after I got my job in Bangor. I love my house. It isn't big and it's a little old, but that's what makes it special. I like how the floor creaks and the smell of old wood and old-fashioned door handles and small windows and the wraparound porch. I planted flower gardens, too, but there are a lot of weeds. Now that I don't have to work, I'll have all the time I need to take care of them. They should be beautiful this summer. Except I kind of miss the way it was before. Working, I mean. I wouldn't mind a part-time job, but it's hard to find one as an engineer.

I was working sixty-hour weeks. I don't miss that." She stopped, trying to keep from meeting his direct gaze, aware that she'd let go a lot of chatter. "Where do you live?"

"I have an apartment in Washington, D.C."

"Do you like it there?"

"It's a place to sleep. I'm not there much."

She nodded. "Right. Sniper." She lifted her glass and drank, looking out at the boats. He didn't say anything so she kept herself occupied sipping more wine.

Their food arrived and she welcomed the excuse to keep avoiding him. She could almost hear his thoughts. Her withdrawal convinced him she couldn't accept his profession. His wife had left him because he was never home. And wouldn't she wind up doing the same? She wanted to make a family. She wasn't interested in a brief affair.

After a few bites, she abandoned the swordfish for the wine, pushing her plate out of the way to prop her elbows on the table. She held the glass with both hands and sipped.

Elam had stopped eating, too. He was looking at her again. Hungry and curious and shrewd all at the same time. What a shame he didn't live closer to her and have a regular job. Why did he have to be a sniper with a phobia of commitment?

"What made you join the Army?" she asked, putting her empty glass down onto the table.

He leaned forward to lift the bottle of wine and refilled her glass. She raised her eyebrows as she met the look of challenge in his eyes. She smiled.

"A cop took pity on me," he said.

"A cop?" She lifted the glass and sipped.

"He arrested me so many times that he finally sat me down and had a long talk with me about the Army. I didn't listen at first, but he kept badgering me until one day I woke up and realized it wasn't such a bad suggestion. I could learn how to use weapons and blow things up."

"You were arrested a lot?"

"More times than I can count."

"For what?"

"Fighting, mostly."

"And you liked the idea of blowing things up."

"I was a boy."

"Sounds to me like you were a troublemaker."

"The cop was my only role model. I never knew my dad."

She knew what it meant to grow up without a parent. Foster parents who did it out of obligation or pity didn't count.

"Why didn't you know your dad?"

"He died when I was young."

"What was your mom like?" She was always fascinated by real moms.

The affection in his eyes clouded with sorrow. "She died in the World Trade Center bombing."

As the shock hit her, Farren sucked in a breath. "Oh, my God." She put down her glass when the liquid sloshed around and came dangerously close to spilling. "I'm so sorry."

"The sad truth is, she worked long hours and wasn't happy. She had a really hard life. Never had a chance."

She studied him, seeing his sadness and maybe a little guilt. "Is that why you do what you do? Fight terrorists outside the law? Nothing stops you from doing what you have to do to take them down. Are you doing it to avenge your mother's death?"

"Does that bother you?"

"Did you go to work for Cullen after your mother died?"

"Yes."

That said it all. "Is that why you do it? Because of your mother?"

"I suppose so."

It didn't bother her that he fought terrorism, but the act of killing outside the law did. But she'd keep that to herself.

"You were lucky to have someone like that cop in your life," she said to redirect the conversation.

A wry grin lifted one side of his mouth higher than the other. "Didn't you have anyone like that growing up?"

She scoffed. "In a foster home?"

"Surely there had to be someone you were close to."

"No. And I wasn't very tough. Unfortunately, that's what I needed to be to grow up in that house. My foster parents' son picked on me all the time. I was overweight and shy and extremely lonely. It wasn't until I grew up and went to college that I started to get tough."

"You still aren't very tough." His expanding smile revealed his teasing.

"Maybe not in your world. But I do know how to stand up for myself."

He didn't say anything for a while. "Have you ever been married?"

"No, but I tried four times."

"You were *engaged* four times?"

"Yes." She cringed with an exaggerated frown.

His eyes crinkled with humor. "What happened?"

"Either they cheated on me or changed their minds."

"I find that hard to believe. What men wouldn't want you?"

"The wrong ones. That's my problem. I keep choosing the wrong men."

He immediately fell silent. Farren almost asked him what he was thinking, but the feeling that he was another one of those wrong men kept her from asking. Instead, she drank wine and talked about little things. Movies. A shopping excursion with her neighbor. A chat forum she'd participated in.

By the time she finished her third glass of wine, she knew it was time to leave. She wondered if she was slurring her words.

Elam stood first. She used the table to push herself up, stumbling as she straightened and moved away from the table. He caught her around the waist and she found herself pressed against him.

"Whoa." She looked up at his face, melting inside from more than the soft buzzing in her head.

"Can you walk?" he asked.

She pushed away from him. "Of course." On sheer willpower, she led him through the maze of tables and out of the restaurant.

Outside, Elam walked beside her. He offered his elbow and she smiled and slipped her arm under his, her hand draping over his forearm.

"You're awful gentlemanly for somebody who shoots people for a living."

"I don't want you to trip in those shoes."

"A likely excuse for keeping your hands on me." She could feel the side of her breast against his arm. He probably could, too.

The wine made her feel unguarded and warm and tingly. She leaned closer to him as they walked, then tipped her head to see him. His eyes smoldered with responding heat. Would it be so bad if she slept with him? So they'd part ways in a while. Why couldn't she have a little fun?

Because in the end, it wouldn't be fun. If she had sex with him, she'd want more in the morning. She'd want a real re-

lationship. *Crumbs. Remember the crumbs.* They weren't
enough to feed her hunger for a husband and a family.

Still, she felt good being with him, feeling him close.
Wrong or not, she wanted him.

Chapter 5

He's wrong for me. He's wrong for me. Farren kept repeating this in her mind as they headed for the hotel across from the marina. Elam moved his arm around her waist as they crossed the street. Flames licked deep in her core. She stumbled once but no one could convince her it was from the wine. His strength and solid form kept her from looking too ungraceful.

In the hotel, Elam took her hand and led her through the lobby to an elevator. It was getting late so they were alone for the ride up to their floor.

Elam stood next to her, having let go of her hand. She looked at his profile. He turned. His eyes hadn't lost that intimate heat. God, she wanted him. *He's wrong for me.*

But she couldn't stop herself from falling into his gaze. She couldn't look away. And she was afraid her building desire showed in her eyes.

His expression darkened with desire. He turned to face her, stepping closer, as if drawn by an unspoken invitation.

Yes.

He's wrong for me.

He took another step. She reached for his hands and pulled him the rest of the way. He angled his head and kissed her. Putting her hands on his chest, she pushed him against the adjacent elevator wall. Looping her arms around his neck, she pressed her body to his. He slid his hands around her waist and cupped her behind, kneading and moving her over his erection.

She pulled away from the kiss to suck in more air while he kissed her neck just below her ear and moved on to her jaw. He found her mouth and kissed her long and deep. Farren felt drunk with sensation.

He ended the kiss as the elevator doors opened. She didn't care. All she wanted was him, to know that he wanted her, even if it was just this one time. Who cared if it went against her greater goal?

She rose to her toes and kissed him some more.

"Farren," he said against her mouth.

"Mmm." She kept kissing him, tasting him. "Tell me you want me."

He lifted her and put her away from him. For a second she thought he'd refuse her. But he took her hand and pulled her down the hall to their room, his strides long and purposeful. Laughing, Farren trotted to keep up with him. At the door to the room, she ran her hands over his arms and shoulders while she leaned against his body. He opened the door. She stumbled inside after him. He kicked the door shut and she wrapped her arms around him again.

"Say it," she whispered against his mouth. "Say you want me."

"I want you."

The hunger in his raspy voice washed through her. She closed her eyes. It felt so good to be wanted by a man. *By this man.*

"Kiss me. Show me."

He did. He ravaged her mouth until their breathing grew loud in the room.

She lifted her leg, bending her knee beside his hip as she ground her pelvis against him. He swore against her mouth.

"Are you sure?" he rasped. "Are you sure?"

"I'm so sure." She kept kissing him.

He groaned. Then gradually his kissing eased in intensity until he pulled away.

She leaned back and looked up at his face.

"I don't think you are," he said.

He put his hands on her waist and pushed.

She stepped back from him. "What's wrong?"

"I think you'd regret it in the morning."

"No, I wouldn't."

The battle between taking what she offered and restraint burned in his eyes. "You've been drinking."

"Three glasses of wine. I'm not that drunk."

"Farren…"

Maybe he needed more convincing. Maybe she did, too. Something in her warned not to go where the fire in her would lead. But it was too strong. He made her feel so good. She didn't want to stop.

She started to move toward him.

He put his hands on her arms. "Don't, Farren."

His rejection deflated her. She'd just thrown herself at him the same way she had with other men she thought wanted her but in the end didn't. How could she be so stupid? Why did she keep making the same mistakes over and over?

"If I thought you were really okay with this, we'd already be in bed," he said.

He was only trying to be nice now.

Stepping out of reach of his hands, she hugged herself. "I had this friend once. She was really petite and in shape and beautiful. She had a great little house in Maine, an older one. I love old houses. They're small and the rooms don't have much space and the storage is, well, there is none, but I just love the charm. Anyway, this friend of mine dated lots of men but never settled for one. I met a few of them. She was really pretty and the men were all great-looking. But some were really nice, you know?" She paused to make sure he was listening. He watched her with an unreadable expression. "Anyway, I kept wondering why she never settled on one of them. She was going through a nasty divorce when I first met her. No kids, thank God. I think all they had to fight over was the cat. Or maybe it was the bird. She had a bird, too. A love bird that chirped all the time. She liked to let it out of its cage and it would land on your shoulder. I used to wait for it to crap on my clothes. It never did though. That bird had a personality." She turned to Elam. "Do you believe that animals have personalities?"

"I've never owned a pet." Hearing sympathy in his tone, she felt a lump of emotion climb into her throat. She swallowed it away.

"You don't watch movies, you don't listen to music, and you don't have a pet."

"I'm never home."

"So I keep hearing. You have no life, you do realize that, don't you?"

"What happened to your friend?"

"She finally settled. Moved to California to live with her boyfriend. I went to the wedding. Just last fall."

"She settled, huh?"

"Yes."

"What's that supposed to mean?" he asked.

If he didn't get it, she wasn't going to explain. "You're right. I'd regret sleeping with you." She went to her suitcase and grabbed a nightgown before marching into the bathroom. "I hope you find the floor comfortable. There's only one bed, and I'm sleeping in it."

She slammed the bathroom door shut. Every man she'd been with, she'd settled when she could have done better. Elam didn't feel like someone she'd settle for. Elam was so wrong for her. She'd be a fool to let herself fall for him. Yet, the pull in her heart was stronger than any she'd ever felt. *Not fair. Not fair at all.*

So, there was a point to her chatter after all. Elam folded his arms behind his head and smothered a scoff. He'd kept his jeans on and lay on top of the covers on the bed. *Settled.* Did she really think she'd be *settling* if she slept with him? He was tempted to show her just how wrong she was. After the way they'd almost combusted tonight, how could she even think it? Would she still feel like she was settling after he had her?

She talked too much and she was too girly, but he damn well wanted her. The thought of sinking into her, imagining how good it would feel, made him struggle with his conscience. Damn the wine.

The bathroom door opened and Farren emerged, covered from her chest to her knees.

"You aren't sleeping there," she said, stopping beside the bed.

"I'm not sleeping on the floor."

"Elam—"

"Just get in bed, Farren. We've already established nothing's going to happen tonight."

Her lips tightened with annoyance. "Yes, you did make that *perfectly* clear."

She climbed into bed with jerky movements. When she lay on her back under the covers, it was all he could do to keep from tossing the covers back and rolling on top of her.

"I lived in Boston while I was seeing Payton. Did I already tell you that?" She sounded mad. And he sensed another round of chatter coming.

"No," he said, deciding to go along with it. "Who's Payton?"

"He's the politician I almost was stupid enough to marry. Boston is nice, but it's so busy. And it's full of stuck-up people. Not friendly like Mount Desert Island. It's quaint and quiet and beautiful. I am so lucky to live there.

"There's something about Maine I love. It's got a lot of history and it's woodsy and charming. My house was built in 1920. I renovated it. I painted it white and hung black shutters. I told you about the wrap-around porch with shrubs and flowers planted around it. There are planters on the railings, too. Sometimes I just sit on the porch and watch the ocean. There's no beach, just a rocky shore, but it's so beautiful."

So far he could find no hidden meaning in what she was saying. But as she talked, her anger softened. He could hear the love for her home in her voice. It wasn't the first time he'd noticed.

"My kitchen and living room are small. I was careful about the kind of furniture I bought. Nothing too big and bulky, and I wanted an old-fashioned look. It's an old farm-house. I am particular about antique furniture. I didn't want it to look like I went to the flea market for furniture." She laughed a little. "That made it a challenge to find what

I liked. But it was fun. Each new piece of furniture was like a treasure I found, because I knew it was going to fit the décor I was after. It was me, you know? When I'm home, I feel like me."

As opposed to being here, with him, where she didn't. There was her point. "It sounds nice," he said.

"I miss home." The way she said it slammed him. So quietly and with so much emotion. When she returned home, she'd be away from him. Her life would be normal again and she wouldn't have to deal with any of this. *With him.*

To hell with it. He couldn't finish this night without making sure she knew just how much he wanted her.

Rolling to his side, he lifted himself up onto his elbow. Her eyes were closed and her breathing was slow and even. He watched her sleep for a while.

How had it happened that such an angel appeared in his life? Her sweetness drugged him. It tempted him. It also made him want things that would never come to be. Best that she had fallen asleep.

In the morning, she'd realize what a mistake she'd almost made. She'd remember that he was a sniper who worked outside the law. He couldn't offer her what she was looking for. She didn't want to settle for the wrong man again, and he didn't want to *be* the wrong man again.

Elam woke to his satellite phone ringing. He reached over to the side table and answered.

"You're not going to believe this."

"Good morning to you, too, Odie."

"It's after ten at night here."

"What have you got?"

"Jared Fenning was an arms dealer who'd been doing a good job hiding behind his shipping company."

Elam sat up on the bed. So the man who'd threatened Farren for three million had been working with an arms dealer. Terrorists buying arms at that price definitely got his attention.

Farren stirred beside him, rolling onto her back. The nightgown had twisted around her and molded to her gorgeous breasts.

"Who was Jared getting the weapons from?"

"Marc Betts, of Betts International, an arms supplier. Cullen convinced Fenning's lawyer to tell him about their friendship. Apparently they go way back. Betts used Fenning's shipping company on a regular basis. Fenning had offices all over the world and frequently routed shipments through the United Arab Emirates."

"So the shipments look legitimate."

"Right. He complicated the supply chain that way. He probably also used forged end-user certificates to avoid getting caught violating embargo restrictions."

"Anything else?" He doubted Odie had called just to tell him that.

"The lawyer also gave Cullen the name of Betts's last mistress. She wasn't real happy he let her go, so she was a fountain of information."

"I'm not going to ask how Cullen got the lawyer to talk."

Odie laughed briefly. "In his own convincing way. Anyway, the woman told him about a meeting Betts had with Fenning. They were talking about a deal with a man named Imaad al Rasoon. She said they discussed how to get the shipment to Fenning, who said he'd 'take care of the sale from there.' She said the shipment was supposed to happen the week after Fenning was killed."

Elam froze inside while the implications of this news assembled in his mind. "Imaad al Rasoon is one of the men

Ameen listed on the yacht charter documentation in Bodrum. He's coming to the festival."

"Okay, now we're getting somewhere," Odie said, "Imaad's got solid ties to al Qaeda and is climbing his way into Most Wanted land from what I've gleaned in my research. He's got himself a splinter cell, like we thought Ameen had, only this guy seems to have connections all over the place."

"Farren said the man threatening her was in the United States. How'd he get there if he's on our radar?"

"Who knows. But he must have found a way. Don't fool yourself into thinking our borders are impenetrable."

"I don't." That's why he left the States to fight terrorism. He wanted to get them before they found a way onto American soil.

"Anyway, it's clear enough from all this that Imaad is your man. He was working with Fenning. The deal never went through because Fenning's wife shot him before it took place. He's out three million and your girlfriend has all the money."

"Yeah, but why's he going to Marmaris?" Elam asked.

"That's your job to find out," Odie said, but he'd only been thinking aloud. "You need to be extra careful with this one, Elam. Your girlfriend is tit-deep in big trouble if a guy like Imaad is after her. Even if she gives him the money, he'll probably want her dead. Take him out and all her problems will go away."

"I'm on it," he said.

"Your crew will be arriving this afternoon. Sit tight until then. They'll meet you on the yacht."

"Thanks, Odie."

"What are you going to do in the meantime?" she asked in a leading tone.

Elam turned to see Farren's beautiful amber eyes blink open. "I'll give you another six months before that dinky mountain town drives you crazy," he said into the phone, watching Farren grow more aware of him watching her.

"Going to ignore that one, huh?" Odie laughed.

Pretty much, he thought without answering.

"Is she in bed with you?" Odie pressed.

The woman was incorrigible. "There's only one bed in the room."

"That makes it easy for you. Does she know you're neurotic about serious relationships?"

"I'm not neurotic."

"You guys are all the same. That's why I never get tangled up with any of you."

"You're a wise woman, Odie."

"Be kind to her. She's a civilian who doesn't understand your warped mind."

"Thanks for the advice."

"I'll e-mail you a photo of Imaad." Odie disconnected.

Shaking his head, he put the phone back on the bedside table.

"Someone from TES?" Farren asked.

His sharp look must have indicated he wondered how she knew.

"Meryem told me."

"I'll have to be careful what I say around her from now on."

"Did you find anything out?"

"Jared was an arms dealer. His shipping company was a front." He came down onto his elbow, facing her.

Her gaze ran down his chest and back up into his eyes. She pulled the blankets closer to her chin.

Figures, now that she wasn't tipsy on wine, she wanted nothing to do with him.

"Did we kiss in the elevator or was that a dream?" she asked.

He smiled a little ruefully. "We kissed in the elevator."

"I was hoping I dreamed it. You know how that is. You dream something and it seems so real but it isn't and you can't remember everything but it sticks with you all day and you can't stop thinking about it even though you try and it bothers you that you can't be sure it was real and—"

"I can assure you, it was real."

She studied his face, especially his eyes. "You're enjoying this."

"I'm a guy."

"I'm sorry. It won't happen again."

He should be glad, but instead he wished she hadn't said that. "I'll leave that up to you."

"Thank you for not taking advantage of me."

"No need to be so polite." First she was sorry, now she was thanking him.

"It definitely would have been a mistake."

"A big one," he said, keeping his disappointment to himself.

He climbed off the bed and went to boot up the laptop he'd brought with him to take a good look at Odie's e-mail.

Farren followed Elam aboard *Rapture*, the beautiful ninety-five-foot Astondoa he'd chartered for their voyage to Marmaris. She was still so embarrassed. Last night's groping episode wouldn't stop replaying in her head. What was the matter with her? Why couldn't she stop herself from being so desperate? When she saw the name of the yacht, it was all she could do to keep her face from turning red. She could barely look at him, much less figure out how she was going to spend time with him on a boat called *Rapture.*

Stepping onto the aft deck, she followed him past a festive blue-and-white striped alfresco dining area on their way into the salon. An elegant pale leather seating area opened to a curving onyx-topped wet bar. Splashes of bright blue and green and muted gold were a little too much for her taste but she wasn't complaining. It *was* a nice yacht. Despite the name.

A woman emerged from the galley. She was tall, probably five-eight, and slender, but very fit and strong. Her long dark hair was up in a ponytail. She wore no makeup, but her stunning deep blue eyes didn't need any. Her direct gaze moved from Farren to Elam as she approached.

"Haley," Elam said as he took her hand.

"Hello, Elam. I'm your cabin attendant for the voyage." She looked at Farren and stuck out her hand. "Haley Engen."

"Farren Gage." Farren shook the woman's hand.

Haley withdrew her hand and stepped back. There was something about her, something in her body language that said, *Stay back, don't even try to get close to me.*

"Haley is our intelligence analyst. She can also shoot a pistol and fight better than anybody I know."

Haley smiled at Farren. "Elam is exaggerating."

The warmth in that smile brought one to Farren's face.

"We have a bet going at the office," Haley said. "Odie started it."

"You don't even have to tell me," Elam said.

"Who's Odie?" Farren asked Haley.

"Our intelligence officer. But don't ever call her that to her face."

"Odie has a vivid imagination," Elam said.

What was the bet? Farren wondered, but had an idea it was about her and Elam.

A sound at the salon door made Farren look there. Two men approached, both tall and big like Elam and about the same age.

"Yes, but she's usually right," the first one said. His smile lit up his rugged face, but barely reached his shrewd light green eyes. He had a confident swagger she was beginning to think came with the profession. Seeing how big the second man was, she decided their size came with it, too. She felt cornered in the spacious salon. They took up so much room.

"That's why I keep all my girlfriends a secret," the second man said, his grin brightening his dark blue eyes.

The first man stopped beside Haley and said to Farren, "I'm Travis Todd, your captain." He nodded to the guy next to him, "and this is Keenan McKelvers, your chef. The two of us will double as deck hands, too."

Haley reached up and brushed the dark strands of hair that had fallen in front of the captain's eyes. He turned his head with surprise toward her. "You don't look like a captain," she said, lowering her hand. "You look like a pirate."

"Which do you prefer?" He grinned suggestively, but the wiggle of his eyebrows made it clear he was teasing.

She smiled with mock sweetness. "Neither."

"I don't know why the two of you don't start dating," Keenan said. He looked at Farren. "Travis won't let Haley go on any missions if he isn't there with her. They're inseparable but neither will admit it."

"That isn't true. Travis doesn't go on all my missions on purpose," Haley protested. "Do you?"

Travis frowned in a guilty way.

Haley scoffed. "Cullen lets you get away with that?"

"I don't go on all your missions."

"The only ones he doesn't go on are the ones he thinks

aren't dangerous," Keenan said. "Like that time you did an analysis on that water treatment plant."

Haley's jaw dropped and she grunted. "You have been on a lot of my missions. Maybe I should have a talk with Cullen."

"You need somebody to watch over you," Travis said.

She put her hands on her hips and cocked one higher than the other. "And why is that?"

"You know why. You're too full of vengeance. It makes you careless sometimes. I don't want to see you get hurt. Or worse."

"That's very chivalrous of you, Travis. Except I don't need your protection. I can probably kick your ass."

"She probably can." Keenan chuckled.

"Well, we'll never know because I am never going to fight a woman."

"Let's talk about our plans," Elam interrupted. "When we get to Marmaris, the three of you will play the crew and Farren and I will be the happy couple going to a yacht festival."

Alarm prickled Farren.

"Aboard *Rapture*." Keenan chuckled again and looked pointedly at Elam. "You arrange that on purpose?"

"I'm not that creative," Elam quipped.

"Wait a minute," Farren said. "Nobody said anything about role-playing."

"It's just for appearances," Haley said.

Farren looked at Elam, but he kept his expression blank.

"I didn't think you were serious when I heard you on the phone," she said.

"We can't have anyone finding out why we're here," Travis explained. "Even if Ameen got word to his friends that Elam was chasing him, they still won't know who he is or who he's working for."

Farren looked from one waiting face to the next and despaired.

"You don't have to do anything you aren't comfortable doing," Haley said. "As long as you keep up the appearance of being a couple, that's enough. Our biggest worry is keeping the team secret. We have to protect the team."

Farren moved her gaze back to Elam. She couldn't tell what he was thinking. His face was as deadpan as the rest of them, except his pale blue eyes were more familiar to her.

"You have to agree to this or it won't work," Travis pushed.

"All right," Farren reluctantly said. "I'll do it."

"Good. Let's get this boat moving." He glanced at the splashes of blue and gold around him. "Could it be any gaudier?"

"Dinner will be ready at seven," Keenan said.

"I'll keep Keenan company in the galley," Haley chimed in.

"I'll be on deck," Elam said. "I want to make sure no one follows us."

"Good idea. I'll help you from the flybridge," Travis said.

Farren's plans were far less strategic. "Maybe I'll start playing my role and act like this is a vacation. Read for a while." She checked her fingernails. "Change the color of my nails." She looked up at Elam and the rest of them and smiled. "Have a margarita later."

"There's something better than that," Haley said, still smiling. "There's a Jacuzzi in the master suite. Come on. Before I help Keenan I'll show you around and bring you whatever you need. I am the cabin attendant, after all."

In the master suite, Haley led her into the bathroom and started to show her how to run the Jacuzzi. Farren wasn't paying attention.

"What's with Odie's bet?" she asked.

Haley straightened and took a minute before she said anything. "She just likes to tease Elam. He's sort of got a reputation." Her eyes surveyed Farren. "For dating women who are tougher than you appear to be."

"Tougher?"

"Just…like…military women."

"Elam's dated military women?"

"A few here and there."

Of course, how would he have time for more than that? "Were you in the military?"

"Army." Her voice was clipped. Farren wondered if that was a subject that was off-limits.

"Did you date Elam?"

She laughed briefly and without humor. "No."

"Did he want to date you?"

"He asks every woman out on a date who he thinks is tough enough for him."

"What do you mean?"

Haley seemed to debate how much to say. "Elam's wife was a lot like you."

"Not tough?" Should she be insulted?

"No. I don't mean it like that. What I mean is you're…" She twirled her hands as she took in Farren's small-print floral sundress. "So feminine."

"Feminine?"

"Yeah. Ever since his wife left him, he's made a point to avoid women like her." She paused. "Do you know about his wife?"

Farren nodded and looked down at her carefully manicured fingernails. No wonder he thought it would have been such a big mistake to have sex with her. He didn't want to fall for another woman like his wife. Didn't he know that not all women were the same? Just because she was feminine didn't mean she wasn't strong enough to handle his line of work.

Catching herself wanting to prove him wrong, she gave herself a mental shake. She refused to risk another rejection on the hope that he'd feel enough for her to change his mind. But the situation with Elam was unlike the ones with the men in her past. She'd thought the men she'd almost married wanted her. With Elam, there was no doubt he didn't. Not long-term anyway.

Chapter 6

Standing portside at the bow, Farren watched Marmaris grow bigger as they approached. Pine-covered hills under a hazy blue sky sloped down to the water's edge. Deep, clear water shimmered turquoise in the sunlight. Marmaris Bay opened to a bustling shoreline and Netsel Marina. Masts and sails painted a picturesque foreground. She could see the remains of the city's infamous Ottoman castle to her left, surrounded by the original restored buildings of historic Marmaris.

The yacht sailed into the marina. Farren scanned the maze of boats, searching for one called *Lucky,* but it was impossible to read all their names. Travis maneuvered *Rapture* so the stern backed to the dock between two other yachts. She slid her hand along the rail as she walked, searching. Banners and flags signified the location of the boat show at the municipality quay, where charter companies and brokers would flaunt their best models.

Casual but elegantly dressed women and men wandered the marina. More milled along the docks, on and off the boats on display. It was such a happy environment. Happy but tinged with the stench of too much money. She was beginning to hate money.

Oh, how she missed her house in Maine.

"Will you come with me to register?"

She turned to see Elam standing in tan slacks and a short-sleeved white golf shirt, his chocolate hair waving in a slight breeze, eyes hidden by sunglasses.

"For appearances," he added.

Right. "Sure. Fine." Looking down at her sundress, she wondered if she should change.

"You look good."

His words came unexpected and made her jerk her gaze back to him. Their farewell kiss floated through her, followed by what had almost occurred last night. She lowered her eyes and went to him.

"Put this somewhere on your body."

She looked at his palm and took the small, chiplike device from him. "What is it?"

"A GPS receiver with a transmitter."

She raised her eyebrows at him.

"In case I lose you."

"You're afraid you might?"

"No." He hesitated. "Yes."

No, because he was confident in his abilities. Yes, because he didn't want the tragedies of his past to repeat. If something happened to her, he'd have to carry that with him along with his other losses. She looked down at her sundress. No pockets. She glanced at Elam as she tucked the device inside her bra. His eyes heated a little as he watched her. Then he extended his hand.

As she took it, her system suffered another jolt as he led her to the stern and off the yacht.

Walking beside him on the dock, Farren tried to focus on the array of elegant yachts and the people they carried. But Elam's presence surrounded her, warmed her. A beautiful woman in a black one-piece swimsuit with a sheer black sarong wrapped around her held a flute of champagne and looked at them as they passed. Her thick black hair was clipped in a messy pile on top of her head and she wore dark lipstick.

Beyond that yacht, Farren saw another moving through the water. She barely caught sight of the name.

Lucky.

She gave Elam's hand a tug. He looked with her but the yacht disappeared in the tangle of other vessels.

"Yeah, we saw it," Elam said.

Farren looked at him. He sounded like he was talking on a phone but he wasn't holding one.

He grinned and tapped his ear.

She realized he was wearing an inconspicuous earpiece and was talking to the crew on *Rapture*.

"We'll get a closer look," he said. "See if we can spot the *Sea Minstrel*, too."

Elam guided her to the registration desk. After filling out some paperwork, they walked back along the dock.

"Haley says *Lucky* docked somewhere along here," Elam said.

Farren spotted the sleek lines of the yacht almost at the same time. "There." She gestured with her head.

He put his hand on her lower back and guided her closer. He slowed his pace, making her do the same.

No one was on deck. Farren thought she caught movement inside the salon. Someone came out on deck but disappeared along the portside.

"Let's head back," Elam said.

They had to walk along the shore to reach their dock, passing a line of shops and kiosks on their way, weaving around the throng of people.

Back aboard *Rapture,* she followed Elam to the flybridge, where Travis held a pair of binoculars and Haley crouched low with a camera, clicking pictures. Keenan pretended to be working on deck, but it was obvious to Farren he was on the lookout for anything suspicious.

"We found *Sea Minstrel,*" Travis said, handing Elam the binoculars. "Two docks over from *Lucky.*" He pointed.

Elam searched with the binoculars. When he stopped moving them, Farren knew he found it.

"Haven't seen anyone yet," Travis said.

Haley straightened. "Someone's on the deck of *Lucky.*" She snapped pictures. "Wait a minute… He looks familiar." She lowered the camera and looked at the display.

Elam leaned closer. Farren moved to Haley's other side.

She recognized the man. "That's Congressman Shay."

Haley and Elam shot gazes her way and Travis took the binoculars from Elam to seek out the congressman's yacht.

"My ex-fiancé spoke about him," Farren said. "Colin Shay visits third-world countries to speak out about his anti-terrorist views. Payton said he's in-your-face religious, too. Catholic."

Haley looked from Travis to Elam.

"Did your ex-fiancé know him?" Haley asked her.

Farren shook her head. "No. He just mentioned him. He talked politics all the time." It had made her nauseous. "He talked about a lot of politicians, too. I just remember Shay because he seemed more aggressive than the others."

"I'll confirm his ID. Isn't it interesting that Carolyn Fenning was going to meet a congressman?"

"Especially since her husband was selling arms to terrorists," Travis said, lowering his binoculars. "Very interesting indeed."

"Maybe she learned what her husband was doing," Farren said. "Someone like Congressman Shay could help her."

"Why not just go to the police?"

"Maybe she knew Shay," Elam said. "Trusted him."

"Why come all the way to Marmaris for help?" Haley challenged.

"And start out in Bodrum," Elam said.

The three fell into silent speculation.

"Maybe we should talk to him," Farren said.

"You and Elam should," Travis said. "Let's keep our cover intact. We've got a good view of the yacht from here. We'll have your back if anything goes wrong."

Farren's heart pulsed in an anxious rhythm as she stepped aboard *Lucky* behind Elam.

"Are you sure we should be doing this?" she asked.

"Worst thing he'll do is ask us to leave," he said.

Passing tan chairs and a glass-topped dining table, she stopped with Elam at the salon door. Inside she could see a curving white leather couch and built-in entertainment center. Beyond that, a woman and two teenage children, a boy and a girl, sat at a dining table. The woman looked at least a decade younger than the congressman.

Elam knocked on the glass door. The woman looked over and stood. Reaching the door, she slid it open and looked from Farren to Elam. "Yes?"

"Is Congressman Shay aboard?" Elam asked.

"Who are you?"

"We're here at the festival and noticed he was, too. We'd just like to say hello."

"Just a minute." She closed the door and went to speak to her children. They left the dining area and she followed.

"What do you want?"

Farren jumped and turned to her right. A man armed with a pistol stood there. Another appeared from the starboard side.

"What are you doing aboard this yacht?" the first one demanded.

Elam repeated what he'd told the woman.

"The congressman isn't taking visitors right now. If you give me your names, I'll pass the information along."

"We'd rather—"

"It's all right, Edward. I'll see them."

Farren faced a tall, fiftyish man with salt-and-pepper hair cropped close to his head and hazel eyes surrounded by fine-lined skin. He walked around the other security guard. He had a slight paunch around the middle.

"Have a seat." The congressman indicated the outdoor table. He nodded to the guard standing on the starboard side, who disappeared inside the salon.

Farren sat beside Elam, across from the congressman, eyeing the guard named Edward. He stood in the shadows, leaning against the side of the yacht on the first step leading to the upper deck.

"What brings you here?" the congressman asked. He had clever eyes that didn't hide his curiosity over their purpose. "You didn't come to the festival just to see me, did you?"

"We were in the area," Elam answered cagily. "I'm Elam Rhule and this is Farren Gage."

The congressman turned his gaze to Farren and studied

her. After a moment, he returned his look to Elam. "Am I supposed to know you?"

"Farren's mother was recently shot and killed. Her name was Carolyn Fenning. We were wondering if you knew anything about her death."

The congressman went still, but only for a second. He looked at Farren, then back at Elam. "What makes you think I would know her?"

"She wrote the name of this yacht festival and your yacht on her itinerary," Farren said. "She also included a date and time. It seemed to me she was planning to meet someone here."

The congressman met her gaze and she had to stop herself from fidgeting. He wasn't an easily intimidated man and the way he studied her made her uncomfortable.

"I don't know a Carolyn Fenning. But I'm very sorry for your loss, Ms. Gage," he said, his voice surprisingly gentle.

"I barely knew her," Farren answered, keeping her tone even. "It's hard to think of it as a loss. She abandoned me to marry a man who hated children. I grew up in a foster home."

He seemed to contemplate that for a moment. "Then what brings you halfway around the world on a quest for answers about her death?"

"She left me all her money. I find that strange, since she didn't care enough to keep me."

"Yes, I can see how that would raise some questions. Again, I'm sorry, Ms. Gage. I wish I could help you. I don't know why your mother wrote the name of this yacht."

Farren glanced at Elam, uncertain what to say next. He took her silent cue and faced the congressman. "Did you charter this yacht, Mr. Shay?"

"No. It belongs to my father," he answered. "But we try to keep that secret. Publicity and all."

"Quite a coincidence that Carolyn wrote the name of this particular yacht on her itinerary, don't you think?" Elam pressed.

"Coincidence or not, I can't tell you why she wrote it."

"Can't? Or won't?" Elam said.

The congressman's eyes flared with anger. "I came here with my family, Mr. Rhule. Why would I plan to meet a woman here, at an international yacht festival?"

"She chartered her own yacht in Bodrum," Farren said. "She planned to sail here."

The congressman only looked at her.

"Maybe you planned to sneak out a night or two to be with her," Elam said.

"In such a public environment? I'd have to be a fool."

"Were you having an affair with Carolyn Fenning?" Elam asked anyway.

"No."

"Then maybe you had a different reason for wanting her to meet you here."

"You're beginning to try my patience, Mr. Rhule."

"Were you doing business with her?"

"I told you I don't know a Carolyn Fenning. And I don't appreciate what you're insinuating. I wasn't planning to cheat on my wife, and I don't have any other reason for asking another woman to meet me here. Now, I think I'll have to ask you to leave." He stood and motioned for his security guard to come forward.

The man did, and stood with his hand on the gun holstered at his waist, looking at Elam expectantly.

Elam stood, so Farren did, too.

"One more question, Congressman," Elam said. "Does the name Imaad al Rasoon mean anything to you?"

"Should it?"

"With your reputation as a crusader against terrorism, I'd have a hard time believing it doesn't."

"Who the hell are you?" the congressman demanded.

"I'll take that as a yes."

"Who sent you?"

"I'm just a concerned American citizen who came to be with his girlfriend." He slid his arm around Farren's waist, grinning in a taunting way. Then he guided her off the yacht.

On the dock he stopped and looked at the congressman. Farren looked with him. Shay still stood at the table, watching them with a crease of tension above his nose.

"He's lying," she whispered as they walked down the dock.

"If I were a congressman with his reputation, I wouldn't want news of my mistress reaching the press, either. Especially since she was murdered and her husband was in the middle of an arms deal with a terrorist."

"You think they were having an affair?"

"Yes. But what I don't get is why she planned to come all the way here to meet him."

"Yeah. Maybe she was trying to run away, get as far from her husband as she could. Maybe Congressman Shay was the only one she knew who could help her, and this was the safest place to meet him."

"That would be my guess, too."

The next day, Elam walked beside Farren along a dock at the boat show. All around them were expensive, extravagant yachts and did she notice any of them? Nope.

"I was just minding my own business at the bookstore…" He'd been listening to her chatter for about a half hour now. Sometimes he paid attention. Most of the time he didn't. She wasn't saying anything he couldn't keep up with by half-listening. No hidden meaning in her endless monologue this time. She was just talking about the woman who'd interrupted her to discuss a book she planned to buy.

"Pretty soon she was telling me about her son, how he was diagnosed with leukemia when he was fifteen and ended up dying. That's when I realized she was reaching out to me. We went to have coffee and talked the rest of the afternoon."

He smiled because he could see her doing something like that. Farren was a chatterbox and at first glance seemed to make blonde jokes a reality, but deep down she had an amazing heart and an even more amazing mind.

"She's one of my closest friends now."

Just then a tall, thin man with dark hair caught his attention. He was standing near one of the food kiosks, doing a bad job of trying to fit in with the crowd. His white shirt tucked into khaki pants looked expensive, but his untrimmed beard and flitting gaze gave him away. Elam recognized him from the photo Odie had sent. It was Imaad al Rasoon.

Elam pretended not to notice him and went with Farren to a booth that sold tea. She bought a container of apple tea. He wondered if he should have left her back on the yacht, but he felt better when he had her in his sight. Nobody'd get past him to hurt her. He'd make sure of that.

"This is popular tea here," she said as they moved away.

"I know." He covertly checked Imaad's whereabouts and saw him following.

"I wonder if it's just a tourist ploy," she went on. "Do the locals really drink this stuff as part of a tradition?"

"I'm sure they do. Meryem served it."

"Oh, yeah. It's decaffeinated, can you believe that?"

"Mmm-hmm."

Farren gave his shoulder a playful slap. "You're not listening."

He smiled, not having to pretend, and glad she wasn't, either.

"Let me guess, you don't drink tea," she said.

"I don't drink tea."

"Is there anything you like? Or are you just a machine with skin?"

"I enjoy lots of things."

"Like what?"

He smiled. "You."

That stunned her for a second. "You do not. Come on, what things do you enjoy?"

He could tell she was flirting and damn if he didn't like it. "I don't know. Most anything, I guess."

"When you have time," she mimicked.

"Contrary to what you think, I do like movies and music."

"Really?"

"Really."

"Are you trying to convince me that you're normal? That sounds almost normal."

"You don't think I'm normal?"

"You kill people for a living."

"I stop evil people from hurting innocent ones."

"Noble, but still not normal."

"Is that what you're looking for? Someone normal?"

She looked ahead of them as they walked. "Yeah, I guess so." But she scrunched up her mouth as though the notion didn't appeal to her. "That seems so boring all of a sudden."

"Nothing about you is boring." He checked behind them, pretending to look at a kiosk full of hats as they passed. Imaad still followed.

"Really?"

"Really." He put his hand on her lower back and steered her onto a yacht.

"What about me isn't boring to you?"

"Pretend like you're into this yacht," Elam said brusquely.

She glanced around at the cold interior, white furniture accented by a stiff flower arrangement and little else. "That's going to be hard."

He chuckled.

"What are we doing aboard this terrible waste of good money?" she asked.

A woman wearing a shirt with a yacht charter logo eyed them with distaste.

"You just insulted the saleswoman," he said.

She fingered a spindly branch of the flower arrangement. "You didn't answer my question."

"Everything."

Her warming amber eyes found his over her shoulder. "Everything?"

"Yes."

The way she smiled at him, her face angled to see him, her eyes alight with affection, made him want to kiss her.

When he saw Imaad step into the salon, Elam gave Farren's hand a tug. She twirled toward him just the way he'd intended. Catching her around her waist, he pulled her against him.

"Keep smiling at me like that and I'm taking you back to the yacht," he said.

Her eyes sprang wide and round and her mouth dropped open in alarm.

"Play along," he said low enough for only her to hear.

He heard her faltering breaths but her eyes relaxed a little. "What's wrong?"

"Maybe nothing, but I need to be sure."

She slid her hands up his chest and folded them behind his neck. He fought the flaring heat running through him.

She tilted her head back, putting her mouth under his. Whether or not she intended it to be an offer, he took it as one and kissed her. Feeling her stiffen in his arms, he knew she hadn't. Slanting his mouth over hers, he moved his lips against hers, coaxing until she softened and let him inside.

He kept it brief. Any more and he'd be lost in her. He lifted his head and smiled down at her startled look.

Imaad had moved closer, feigning interest in a painting hanging on the wall to Elam's right.

Farren noticed and leaned back a little, her hands sliding down to his chest.

"Is this your first time in Marmaris?" Imaad asked, his English disturbingly good.

Elam felt Farren's fingers dig into his chest. "Yes. You?"

"Yes." His gaze shifted to Farren. "It is the perfect setting for a...shall we say...rendezvous?"

Elam released Farren to turn and face Imaad fully. "I hear there's quite a nightlife, too."

"I prefer the food, myself."

Elam wondered if there was a point to this small talk.

"You are from the United States, yes?" Imaad asked.

"Yes, we both are," Elam said.

"You are traveling together?"

"We met in Bodrum."

"At the Castle of St. Peter," Farren said.

Elam beamed with admiration for her quick aplomb. Imaad looked from her to him.

"What brings you to Marmaris?" Elam asked.

Imaad's gaze moved back to Farren. "I came to attend to business."

"What kind of business?"

The way Imaad kept looking at Farren suggested she knew what kind of business.

Without responding, he removed a business card and handed it to Farren. She took it from him.

"I will give you until morning." Then he turned and walked away, leaving the salon.

"That's him," Farren said, catching her breath. "He's the one who called me."

"That's Imaad." He read the card. *Three million*, it said. Wire instructions followed.

He grunted. "It isn't going to be that easy, pal."

"What are we going to do?" Farren asked.

He didn't like her frightened look. A woman like her should never have a look like that. "Let's go back to the yacht." Taking her hand, he led her off the show yacht. Outside, he searched around him, doing so surreptitiously in case someone watched.

He didn't see Imaad. He did, however, see someone else. A shorter man, just as thin with a trimmed beard. He wore white slacks with a light blue shirt, but his mannerisms gave him away.

Reaching the marina, Elam looked back. The man still followed, but stopped when they reached the dock leading to *Rapture*.

"Hello, down there," a voice called out.

Elam saw it was the woman they'd passed earlier. She still wore her suit and held a fresh glass of champagne, dark red lipstick marking where she sipped.

"I'm having a few guests for a little sun and hors d'oeuvres. Why don't you invite your captain and stop by in about an hour or two?"

Elam smiled. "Thanks. I think we'll take you up on that." He didn't see much happening the rest of the day anyway. Not unless Imaad and his men made a move before morning, but the rest of his team would be watching.

Besides, the idea of spending the rest of the afternoon with Farren appealed to him. Maybe too much.

"Wear a swimsuit if you want," the brunette called as they passed.

Elam waved.

Haley and Travis were waiting for them when they returned. Climbing the stairs to the flybridge, where they had a view of the entire marina, Farren sat on a bar stool and swiveled to face the other three.

"We're being watched," Elam said.

"So is the congressman's yacht," Travis responded. "Spotted a couple of men casing it. Been doing it for about an hour now."

"Maybe he's the reason they planned to come here," Elam suggested.

"Killing a Catholic congressman who's an outspoken critic of terrorism?" Farren nodded. "That'd make the news."

"There's that," Elam said. "And there's his involvement with Carolyn. She knew something and Imaad doesn't want anyone finding out what it is."

"We've got to get Shay talking. Does he even know the danger he's in?" Haley looked from Elam to Travis.

"Too bad Carolyn can't talk to us from her grave," Elam said.

"So, the question still remains. Why was she coming to Marmaris to meet Shay?"

"We'll get our answers," Elam said. "In the meantime, Farren and I were invited to an afternoon cocktail party aboard the yacht just down the dock from here." He faced Travis. "The host specifically requested your presence."

Travis frowned and his gaze shifted to Haley, who met it with a derisive frown of her own.

"He's been watching her with the binoculars," she said.

"I have not."

"I can tell when they're too low to be trained on Shay's yacht."

He didn't respond and Haley pivoted. "Go ahead, enjoy yourself. The rest of us will stay here and work."

"I'll go, but only to keep up appearances."

"Yeah, right."

Farren changed into her lime-green swimsuit and lamented that she hadn't packed any full-piece suits. Her breasts were too big. They were full and round and her cleavage was way too pronounced. For Elam.

Tying a pink sarong splashed with lime-green martini glasses around her waist, she left her hair down and put a light coat of gloss on her lips. *Not for Elam. It wasn't.* But a tiny voice persisted in her head. *It was for him.*

Taking a deep breath, she grabbed her sunglasses and left the cabin.

In the salon, Elam and Travis waited. They both wore swim trunks and leather sandals and nothing else. Farren couldn't keep her eyes from drinking in the sight of Elam's chest, lightly covered in hair that gathered in a dark line that trailed down to the waistband of his trunks. His legs were long and muscular, but not so much that it ruined his streamlined physique.

Seeing Travis and Haley notice her gaze, she directed her attention away from Elam. "Let's go."

She marched out the door onto the aft deck and then onto the dock, slipping her sunglasses over her eyes just as Elam came in step beside her. Travis walked behind them.

"Helllllo, down there!"

Farren inwardly cringed at the polished woman waving her hand on the aft deck of her glorious yacht. Exotic instrumental music played, soft drums and piano and flute lilting.

She climbed aboard first. A servant appeared with a tray of champagne glasses. She took one.

Four women had chartered the yacht. Two thirtysomething women and their gray-haired mothers. All four were single. One mother was divorced and the other widowed. The brunette, Beverly, or Bev, as everyone called her, was divorced and the redhead, Sara, had never married.

Bev zeroed in on Travis, her eyes gobbling up the sight of him as she went to him. She hugged him longer than was appropriate. Farren watched him give her a flirtatious grin and heard him thank her for inviting him.

"Why do all men do that?" Farren asked.

"Do what?"

"Respond to any woman who shows sexual interest?"

He looked at Travis and Bev. "Because he wants to have sex?"

Farren grunted. "Except you. You seem immune to women who show sexual interest."

He turned his head toward her. "Are you referring to the other night?"

She shrugged. Maybe it wasn't wise to rehash this. She was still embarrassed.

"Don't mistake courtesy for immunity."

"Courtesy?" How appalling! "You were being *courteous* by refusing me?"

"Tell me you wouldn't have regretted it."

She opened her mouth to do just that but stopped. It was true. She would have regretted it. She didn't trust him to be there for her in the long run. And more than that, she was tired of putting her heart on a platter for men. It was the desperate act she'd have regretted. Just because a man wanted her didn't mean he wanted her heart, too.

"See?" Elam said when she didn't answer.

"Would you have regretted it?" she asked.

His smug smile vanished.

"Would you have?" She wasn't going to let him get by without answering.

"No."

"What about it wouldn't you have regretted?"

"Why do women always have to pick things apart like that?"

"Just tell me."

"Sex."

"That's it?"

"What else would there have been?"

She felt her jaw drop as a weighty emotion pulled her mood down. "Right. What else could there have been?" She started to leave the salon. What else could there have been about her that he liked? She was good enough for sex but nothing more. The *everything* he'd claimed wasn't boring about her must only include things that pointed to sex.

On the aft deck, Elam grasped her arm just above her elbow and stopped her. She avoided looking at him as he tugged her to face him, keeping her hands at her sides and standing rigid.

"I didn't mean it like that," he said.

"I want to go back to our yacht." She refused to call it *Rapture* right now.

He let go of her arm and lifted his hand to her chin, cupping it and gently drawing her face so she had to look at him. His eyes were soft with meaning, and apology.

"I didn't mean it like that," he repeated.

She didn't trust herself to say anything. Desperation might make her believe him.

"I did want sex, but the reason I refused you is because I was afraid it would have been more than that and maybe you wouldn't have felt the same in the morning. That maybe you wouldn't have felt the same about this."

Still holding her chin, he pressed his mouth to hers. Farren sucked in a full breath. She hadn't seen this coming. He kissed her so softly. She stood immobile as sensation overwhelmed her. He tasted her. His warm lips moved over hers, taking her lower lip between his, running his tongue over what he'd captured. She opened her mouth with a breathless sound. His hand slid to the back of her head and he kissed her with more purpose. Shivery moments passed.

Then, slowly, he pulled back. His hand slid from her chin and he looked into her eyes.

"Maybe I was wrong," he said, and everything in her heart careened out of control.

It scared her. This was starting to mean too much. Backing away, she turned and stepped onto the dock, hurrying ahead toward *Rapture*.

Chapter 7

The next morning, Farren left her cabin tucked securely in a robe. She hated getting dressed right after climbing out of bed. She liked to have coffee and relax first.

Maybe I was wrong.

She'd thought about what Elam had said and done well into the night. But this morning she'd assured herself that no amount of charm would sway her into sleeping with him. Not when she didn't trust him to stay when this was all over.

She emerged into the salon and saw a rumpled blanket and pillow on the couch. Voices carried from the galley. Farren moved around the wall and entered.

Haley sat with a half-eaten bowl of cereal in front of her. Elam sat beside her, a cup of coffee steaming in front of him. His chocolate hair was messy and his light blue eyes a little sleepy, but they brightened when he saw her.

It sent a shock wave of awareness through her. She was no longer so sure about being immune to his charm. What if he kissed her again?

"Keenan's up on the flybridge keeping watch since Travis decided to take the night off. Breakfast is on your own this morning," Haley said irritably.

After getting herself a cup of coffee, Farren brought a bowl of cereal to the table. Elam pulled back the chair next to him, giving her room to sit. She hesitated, seeing the hooded look of desire stewing in his eyes. When he flashed her a challenging grin, she sat and busied herself eating cereal.

Amazing how he managed to distract her from Imaad's looming threat. The glass door in the salon was visible from the table in the gallery and Farren caught sight of Travis on the aft deck. He entered the blue and gold furnished salon. He wore different clothes than last night, so if he spent the night on Bev's yacht, he'd changed before breakfast. His dark hair was messier than Elam's but his eyes looked rested. Maybe *sated* was a better word.

Farren noticed Haley stiffen and her eyes grow angry as Travis entered the galley. He met her gaze and seemed a little uncomfortable.

"Good morning," Haley said, all but singing the word *morning*.

"Morning." Travis went to the coffeemaker and poured himself a cup.

"Late night, huh?" Elam teased.

Farren elbowed him and he grunted.

Travis brought his cup to the table and looked at Elam, then slowly shifted his gaze over to Haley.

She pushed her spoon around in her bowl of soggy cereal.

"I wasn't aware that I was supposed to be back at a certain time," Travis said.

Haley lifted her eyes and sent him an injured, angry look. "Keenan is up in the flybridge."

"So?"

"So, he's supposed to be *chef,* not your cover whenever you decide to start thinking with your dick."

Travis leaned back on the chair and stared at her. He seemed surprised by her outburst. So was Farren. She'd picked up on some undercurrents between them, but so far their relationship appeared only professional. Granted, she'd seen them flirt, but Haley was always so guarded. She'd given Travis no reason to think she wanted more from him.

"You're upset," Travis said.

"You should have been here doing your job so Keenan could do his."

"You're pissed because Keenan didn't cook breakfast this morning?"

Haley jerked her head down, but not before Farren caught a glimpse of moisture springing to her eyes. Travis saw it, too. He reached over and covered her hand with his. "Hey."

She pulled her hand away. At last she looked up, her eyes pooling now. "It must be so nice for you."

"What must be nice?"

"For it to be so easy."

"What? What's wrong, Haley?"

"It's so easy for you to…" A tear slipped over her lid.

"Haley…"

"Don't bother." She pushed her chair back, the sound of her sob reaching the table as she ran below deck.

With a stunned expression, Travis looked from Farren to Elam.

"What was that all about?" Farren asked.

"I don't know."

"She's been through a lot," Elam said.

"Like what? What happened to her?" Farren asked.

Travis met her gaze. "Five years ago, she was captured in Iraq. She doesn't remember what happened. She only remembers being taken and beaten. She claims she lost consciousness, but...the doctors say they think her mind has blocked the worst of what happened."

It must have been so horrible that now she had trouble with intimacy. Farren's heart cried out in sympathy. "You hurt her by sleeping with that woman."

"I didn't sleep with her. I was out late, but I came back here. Not that it would have mattered anyway."

"What do you mean?"

"Haley and I aren't a couple. We never can be. I don't understand why she's so upset about the idea of me sleeping with someone else."

"Why can't you be a couple?" What was it with these men?

"She needs someone...different from me. Someone who doesn't scare her."

"You don't scare her."

"She's my teammate," he said, too quickly. It revealed his real feelings. He wanted more with Haley; he was just afraid of frightening her. "I don't get personal with teammates. Haley has issues she needs to work out, and I'm not the guy who can help her. I'd only make it worse."

"Why are you so protective of her, then?"

Travis raked his fingers into his hair and held his head. At last he lowered his hands to the table and looked at Farren. "I don't want her to get hurt again."

"Well, I think you gave her the wrong idea by going to Bev's yacht."

"I didn't mean to. I did it for appearances. That's all. A single captain wouldn't come to a festival like this and stay holed up on his yacht with a pair of binoculars." He pushed his chair back and stood. Leaving the galley, he went after Haley.

Farren realized how much she was talking and stopped. Elam sat across from her, relaxed in his chair on the stone patio of the Caria Restaurant. He'd lured her out with the promise of an afternoon of shopping. Wasn't he afraid of what Imaad would do when they didn't do as instructed? No, of course not, but she was.

They'd come here first for a grilled fish lunch and a view of the harbor. With his elbow on the arm of the wicker chair, his forefinger and thumb held his chin and his eyes twinkled with amusement.

"Sorry," she said.

He just continued to look at her.

Feigning nonchalance, she brushed the front of her rust-colored cotton sundress as though there were crumbs there and then looked around the outdoor patio. Colorful flags hung from the second story of the building. Double doors and a window on the first level were open. People filled long rows of cloth-covered tables. Talking surrounded her. She didn't see Imaad anywhere.

"Stop worrying," Elam said.

"Do you think we should go back to the yacht?"

"If Imaad is going to make a move, it won't matter where we are. Don't worry."

"Easy for you to say."

He smiled and started to stand. "Are you ready to go?"

"Sure." She avoided looking at him as she stood with him and walked toward the sidewalk. Elam took her hand. Farren finally looked up at him and saw that he searched their surroundings, ever watchful for Imaad or one of his men. She let him keep her hand.

Shops lined the street and faced the harbor, where boats were moored. The charm of this place had definitely wormed its way into her heart.

When they reached the covered bazaar, Elam let go of her hand. The walkway stretched for as far as she could see and the wares of vendors filled small shops all the way. She caught sight of a rug shop and stopped to admire the Turkish styles and colors. Next was a dress shop. She fingered the silky material of a dark green dress.

Elam leaned a shoulder against the dressing-room wall. He watched her the way he had over lunch. It was starting to wear on her defenses. An undercurrent of sexual energy hummed between them, growing stronger with all the time they were spending together. She rounded a rack of clothes, not moving her gaze from him.

Trailing her hand along the hanging clothes, she smiled as she passed him and left the shop. He pushed off the wall and followed, catching up to her in the long, wide walkway of the covered bazaar.

In the next shop, she bent over a table of handcrafted bracelets. Elam came up behind her. She straightened after she finished studying the pieces and felt his warm breath on her neck. The subtle foreplay set her blood on fire and chased a marvelous shiver across her skin. She turned her head to see him. The corners of his mouth lifted seductively.

What was he doing? Turning up the heat between them on purpose? Or was he as helpless as her against this attraction?

Slipping away from the table, she headed back out into the walkway. Another display of handcrafted jewelry drew her attention. She went into that shop and lifted a pendant in her hand. Elam reached around her and picked up a necklace with a piece of amber dangling from a dark chain. His arm brushed hers.

"It matches your eyes," he said.

She smiled to disguise her leaping pulse.

He clasped the necklace around her neck. His fingers moving her hair out of the way sent another bout of shivers through her. She turned her head. His was right next to hers. He bent to press a kiss to her bare shoulder. Taking in a startled, aroused breath, she leaned her head to the side. He moved his face against her hair and she heard him inhale. A sound escaped her when he slipped his arms around her. His hands spread over her stomach and ribs, pulling her back against him.

He kissed his way up her neck to her jaw. It was a natural thing for her to tilt her head so his mouth could find hers. But before their lips touched, someone interrupted.

"You like necklace, no?"

Elam pulled back with the shop owner's question, and Farren looked up into the fire of his eyes. She couldn't look away.

"We'll take it," he said without breaking their gaze.

But at last, he had to, and went to pay the shop owner.

Outside the shop, Farren couldn't stop looking at him. Every nerve ending in her body tingled. She needed a distraction.

At another dress shop, she veered inside. But the hanging dresses didn't hold her interest. Elam walked on the other side of the rack, staying even with her, his gaze not leaving her. The kiss that they never got to have at the other shop lingered in her mind. She stopped trying to look at dresses and gave in to the fire shooting between them. At the end of the row, she faced him. He moved toward her, eyes burning hotter.

Reaching for her, he grasped her hand and pulled her to him. She closed her eyes when he lowered his head and kissed her. His arms wrapped around her, holding her close. His tongue toyed with hers before sinking deep. She took him, yearning for more. She trembled with need for him to do more.

Digging her fingers into his hair, she held him tight as he kissed her.

Elam lifted his head and looked down at her, breathing as hard as her.

"Let's go back to the yacht," he said.

An image of them naked on her bed, writhing in the act of sex, shocked her.

"Yes" was on the tip of her tongue. She wanted him on top of her, inside her. Moving deep. The strength of her desire shook her. *She wanted him.* She wanted him in a way that made her dizzy. Shivers of sensation consumed her as she imagined him touching her where she needed him.

No. Stop. Where would this lead when it came time for her to go home? To a broken heart, that's where. Elam wouldn't come with her to Maine. He wouldn't be able to leave his job and he wouldn't risk his heart on her.

She felt too much. Already. How would she feel after sleeping with him?

Lost. Hopelessly in love. Was it already too late? Was she falling in love with him? She didn't think she'd ever felt this strongly for anyone.

No. She couldn't let that happen. Love him? The idea frightened her. Pivoting, she hurried out of the shop. Things were careening too far out of her control.

In the walkway, she dodged a couple and their young daughter and broke into a jog, not wanting Elam to catch up to her. She needed to escape the way she was beginning to feel about him. A man stepped into her path. She bumped into him and lost her balance over his feet. He held her and forced her into a shop.

"Hey!" She struggled against his hold. "Let go of me!"

But he dragged her through the shop to the back. She could barely make out the dim interior of the building. But soon she was whisked out a rear door and shoved into the back of a car.

The man spoke rapidly in a language she didn't understand. Struggling, she sat up and looked through the back window. Elam came running out the door just as the car squealed away. He ran after her.

But he wasn't going to catch her.

Cursing himself as he ran down the street, Elam flipped open his phone and called Haley. The car carrying Farren away from him disappeared around a corner. His heart might as well have climbed up into his throat. He'd let his desire go too far.

"Tell me she's got the GPS device on her," he said when Haley answered.

"You lost her?"

"Is she wearing it?"

He listened to her call Travis and Keenan. "Yes," she said to Elam. "She's wearing it."

"I'm just leaving the bazaar. Where is she?"

"Heading down Kemal Elgin Boulevard."

Elam searched for a vehicle. When a man parked along the street, he opened the car door and pulled the driver out. Yanking the keys from the man's hand, he got into the car while the man yelled in Turkish. Elam raced down the street and turned off the boulevard at Haley's instruction.

"There. She's no longer moving." She told him the address. "Don't go in until we get there. Five minutes."

"I'm not waiting."

"Five minutes, Elam."

He disconnected and raced the rest of the way to an old stone villa in a quiet suburb of Marmaris. He recognized the car parked along the side. The lush gardens in the front would have hidden someone forcing Farren inside. Or carrying her. Anger pushed at his control. That and self-disgust. He should have never let this happen.

Farren stumbled as two men pushed her inside a room. She regained her balance and came back to the door as it closed. She tried the handle. It was locked. She slapped the door.

"Let me go!"

Listening to footsteps fade, she turned and faced the room. It was furnished in Turkish style, with colorful pillows adorning the bed and an expensively woven rug at the foot of it. She searched the room. There was nothing to use as a weapon. Not even a lamp. She started toward the window.

The sound of the door unlocking stopped her.

She spun and watched in horror as the door swung open and the man who'd abducted her entered. His face remained unreadable, but she thought she saw anger and repulsion in his dead-looking black eyes.

"Remove your clothes and put these on." He threw a bundle onto the bed beside her.

She looked down at the bland pile then back at him. He closed the door, but stayed in the room with her. Did he intend to watch?

She shook her head.

He walked farther into the room. Fear electrified

Farren's body. She folded her arms in front of her, her fists above the neckline of her sundress. She backed up as he advanced. When she came against a bedside table, she bolted to her right and tried to get past him.

He grabbed her hair and yanked. She lost her footing and landed on her backside. Standing, he straddled her, looking down at her cowering on the floor. She swallowed the begging words that would give away how terrified she was and crawled backward. Her back came against a leg of the table so she veered toward the bed. If she could just get across it, maybe she could make it to the door.

She put her elbows on the mattress and inched her way onto the bed. The man leered at her. With one quick stride, he reached her, bending to grip the front of her sundress. He tore it to her waist. Farren screamed and rolled, crawling on hands and knees across the bed. He grasped her ankle. She kicked free and scrambled to her feet on the other side of the bed. He moved between her and the door.

Whimpers pushed up her throat and made their way past her lips. She held the dress over her bare breasts, shaking violently. She'd had to put the GPS device in her shoe today. Oh, God, she hoped Elam could find her.

The man started toward her. She searched wildly for another escape. The only window was on the other side of the bed. She would never get it open before he caught her. She backed up until the wall stopped her.

The leering man kept coming toward her. His eyes horrified her. So dark and so full of evil hatred. He took hold of her wrists, trying to dislodge her grip on the dress. She brought her knee up and tried to kick him, but he twisted his hips in time to deflect her attempt, never loosening his hold on her wrists. With a yank, he pulled her away from the wall and sent her sailing onto the bed.

Farren tried to crawl to the other side, struggling to keep herself covered at the same time. The man lifted her by the waist and flipped her onto her back. Farren tried to pull the torn material of her dress over her breasts, but he captured her wrists and shoved them roughly above her head. Holding them in one hand, he reached for the hem of her dress with the other, tugging it up her legs. She screamed long and loud, squirming and kicking to no avail. He was wiry but much stronger than her.

Elam drove past the house and parked where he'd be out of sight. Then, watching the stone villa for anyone guarding the exterior, he approached. Checking his surroundings, he slipped his pistol from its holster inside his shirt. Using the gardens as cover, he made it to the side of the house and leaned against the stone wall. Peering around the corner, he held the pistol ready to fire and crouched low to pass unseen beneath one of the front windows. Stone stairs led up to the door. He climbed them and carefully checked the handle. It was unlocked.

Turning the handle, he kicked it wide open and rushed inside, swinging his gun when he caught a movement to his right. Elam fired two silenced shots, putting two holes in the forehead of a tall, dark man whose gun slipped from his hand as he fell in a dead heap to the floor.

A scream from the upper level froze his concentration for a few seconds. *Farren.* His heart plunged with dread.

He had to save her. Now.

Another man rushed him from behind. His distraction cost him. He turned too late. The man, this one shorter and a little heavier than the first, gave his wrist a painful chop. Elam held on to his pistol with one hand and slammed his other fist into the other man's left eye socket. His head jerked backward, but he kicked and got Elam with a knee to his midsection.

Grunting, Elam staggered back and saw the man scrambling toward the fallen man's gun. Elam fired his pistol and got the man in the thigh. He wanted at least one of the men alive to question, and deliver a message.

Two steps and he reached the fallen man's gun. He kicked it out of the moaning man's reach. Bending, he raised his gun, giving the man a good whack on the side of his head. The man went still. Elam would wake him up as soon as he had Farren.

He heard her scream again.

The horrible man had the hem of her dress to her waist now. His voice sounded gutteral as his fingers started pulling her underwear down.

Something crashed outside the door, making him go still.

Farren's throat was raw from screaming and breathing so hard. She writhed her hips in an attempt to throw him off her. She twisted her hands and was begging—pleading for him to stop.

The door banged open, breaking away from its hinges due to the angry force.

The man leaped off her to face the one who entered. She scurried to the corner of the bed, shaking. She felt sick enough to throw up.

A man started hitting her attacker. *Elam.* Elam had found her! He deflected two swings from her attacker and punched one of his own right in the man's face. The man was no match for Elam, who didn't stop hitting his face.

She heard Elam swearing as he threw the man against the wall and strode after him. The man held up his hand as though in surrender. But Elam gave him no mercy. He kicked him in the ribs, then lifted him by his bloody shirt and started punching his face again.

Just when Farren was about to turn away, he finally let the man slump to the floor. The man moaned and rolled onto his stomach, then pushed himself up onto his hands and knees. Blood dripped to the floor as he tried to crawl away.

Breathing hard, Elam turned his head. She met the feral gleam in his eyes as he took in the sight of her cowering on the bed, holding the scraps of her dress over her nakedness. Dark fury blazed with increasing intensity in his eyes.

The man on the floor staggered to his feet and lunged toward Elam. But Elam's reflexes were too fast and he swung his gun in time to stop him with a bullet in his forehead.

Farren covered her mouth with her shaking hand, feeling bile rise in her throat. She felt light-headed and cold.

The bed beside her depressed as Elam sat down. The unmerciful rage in his eyes had calmed. He reached for her, touching her cheek. Gently.

"Are you all right?"

She nodded.

He looked down at her ruined sundress. With a clenched jaw and firmly pressed lips, he pulled his shirt off and put it over her head. She let go of her dress to pull it over her, relieved to be covered.

When she finished, he slid his arms under her and lifted. She looped one arm over his shoulder as he carried her from the room. The villa where the man had taken her was small, but two stories. Downstairs, the main room consisted of a living area and kitchen, both in need of upgrading. A man lay on the floor in the kitchen, his eyes blank. Two holes darkened his forehead and blood that had stopped flowing trailed to the tiled floor. In the open but sparsely furnished living room, another man lay. He stirred, groaning. Blood oozed from a gunshot wound in his thigh. The sight made her feel sick all over again. Too much violence. She'd almost been raped. It was all beginning to overwhelm her.

Elam set her down on her feet. She swayed when his support left her and put her hand on her stomach, wondering if she was going to throw up. She swallowed a few times and tried to keep her breathing even.

She watched Elam go to the groaning man. He knelt beside him as the man propped himself up on one elbow, blinking, trying to look up at Elam.

"Did Imaad send you?" Elam asked.

The man blinked more. He said something in his language.

"Did Imaad send you?" Elam repeated.

After a lengthy hesitation, the man nodded. He knew English; the attempt at feigning didn't fool Elam.

"What was he going to do with the weapons Jared Fenning was planning to sell him?" Elam asked.

The man stared up at Elam and said nothing.

"What was he going to do?" Elam repeated.

A long moment passed before the man finally shook his head. He couldn't tell them.

Elam didn't force the man to talk. Was he holding back in deference to what Farren had just been through? She'd already seen too much. Endured too much. His chivalry was sweet, but she was still so shaken she couldn't appreciate it fully.

"You tell him he goes through me from now on," he said instead.

"Wire the money and he will leave her alone," the man said.

Elam put his pistol to the man's temple. "If he wants

anything, he goes through me. Make sure you tell him. Because if you don't, I'll come find you and kill you. Understand?"

The man nodded.

Elam swung his gun and slammed it against the man's temple. Farren flinched. The man went limp, unconscious again. She slumped to the floor and sat there until Elam returned to her and picked her up with a muttered curse. He was still so angry.

Outside, there was a car waiting. Haley was behind the wheel. Elam put Farren down and helped her into the backseat. When he sat next to her, he put his arm around her and she snuggled close. Before Haley drove away, Travis and Keenan appeared from each side of the building. Travis climbed in the front passenger seat and Keenan climbed in next to Farren and Elam.

Haley jetted into the street and headed for the marina. Travis twisted around in the front seat, his massive shoulder pressed against the seat as he looked back at Farren. His eyes shifted and he took in Elam. Something silent passed between them.

"She's all right," Elam said. "But if I'd have been two minutes later..." Farren heard the catch in his voice.

"You weren't," Travis said. And he looked over at Haley, who was quiet and didn't move her eyes away from the road.

Farren could tell Travis was wishing he could have saved her the same way. Reminded of the dead-eyed man straddling her and pulling up the hem of her dress, she turned her face to Elam's neck, resting her head on his shoulder. She'd been so sure she was going to be raped. She couldn't protect herself.

Elam moved his head so it rested against hers. Something deep shifted in her. She felt the power of his emotion, how much it had cost him to know he'd let her slip away from his guard. But would that change his resolve when it came to avoiding women like her? She couldn't think about that now. All she wanted was a hot bath. And to know she was safe. Elam made her feel safe.

The car came to a stop in the marina parking area.

"Just leave it here," Travis said.

Farren guessed that meant Haley had stolen it to come after her. She'd thank her later.

After they got out of the car, Elam lifted Farren up into his arms.

"I can walk," she said.

"I don't care," he replied.

She didn't have the energy to argue. She lay her head on his shoulder again, not wanting to see the looks they'd get—her in a sundress with a T-shirt over it and Elam bare-chested with a gun holster. It would be a miracle if the authorities didn't stop them.

Travis led the way down the busy maze of docks. It was a long walk to where the bigger yachts were moored.

As they passed Bev's yacht, Travis didn't even look over when she popped her head up and noticed them.

"Is everything okay?" she slurred, holding a glass of dark liquid. When no one answered, she called, "You come by anytime Travis, darling. We'll pick up where we left off, okay?"

Travis glanced at the drunk woman and then at Haley. Haley's head was stiffly erect, eyes straight forward, mouth pressed tight. Facing forward again, Travis climbed aboard *Rapture* and headed for the flybridge.

"Keenan, help Travis keep watch tonight. I don't want

anybody unwanted getting within fifty feet of this yacht," Elam said.

"They won't," Keenan said. "Not unless they want to answer to me and my pistol."

Without any further acknowledgment, Elam carried Farren to her cabin.

He sat her on the bed, then knelt before her, just looking up at her as if he didn't know what to say.

"I need a bath," she said. "With bubbles."

He smiled but not in a humorous way. It was more affection than anything. Nodding, he stood and went to the bathroom. She heard the water running.

She rubbed her wrists where her attacker had held her. They were sore and a little red, but nothing more.

Before the water shut off, she stood and walked into the bathroom. Her legs felt rubbery. Catching a glimpse of her image in the bathroom mirror, she averted her gaze. She didn't want to see her dress under this shirt. She didn't want to relive the terror.

Elam straightened from testing the water temperature and turned to face her. She looked at the press of his lips and the intensity in his eyes. His anger had subsided but his alertness hadn't. Only instead of looking out for danger, he seemed more aware of her, wary of her, uncertain what to do next. He stuffed his hands into his jean pockets.

She should ask him to leave the bathroom now. She should take a bath alone. Except she was still so vulnerable from what had happened. The thought of being alone gave her a sinking feeling, while the thought of him staying with her was like a ray of sunshine brightening her from the inside out.

"I don't want to be alone," she said.

He stared at her.

"Please…"

Without moving his eyes, he shrugged out of his gun holster and put it on the bathroom counter.

Farren turned her back to the mirror and pulled Elam's T-shirt off her, next came the sundress. She heard him put his shoes aside. She kicked hers off but left on her underwear. Elam stepped into the tub and sat, still in his jeans, opening his arms. She stepped into the tub and sat between his legs.

Leaning back, she used him as a backrest. He carefully wrapped his arms around her. The sweetness of it washed her soul. She melted inside. He reached to their right and pressed a button. Jets came on, sending bubbles to the surface.

"I couldn't find any bubble bath," he said.

Farren closed her eyes and turned her head into the curve of his neck. "It's okay."

His arms held her snugly to him. *He'd saved her, this sniper who'd hardened his heart to love.* She closed her eyes, secure and warm and lulled into enchanted serenity. She wouldn't think about how much she wanted to find a way inside his armor. How much she wanted to be the woman who made him love again. No, for now she'd savor his nearness. She'd worry about the rest later.

Chapter 8

Elam woke to find Farren's head resting under his chin, her tangle of blond hair covering his shoulder and chest. Her hand lay on his abdomen. Her smooth bare leg was entwined with his rougher ones. He'd taken off his wet clothes last night and now wished he'd at least gotten dry ones from his duffel bag. Unable to stop himself, he lifted his head to get a better view of her. Her nightgown was hiked to her waist and the fresh pair of underwear she'd changed into after their bath pressed against his naked hip.

He dropped his head back onto the pillow and looked up at the ceiling, swallowing a groan. Any more of this and he was a goner.

She moved, a long, languid stretch. He felt all her soft parts slide against him and did groan, a strangled sound that was more of a grunt. The feel of her intoxicated him. He could smell her, too. All woman.

She stiffened. Lifted her head. Sleepy amber eyes widened into full alertness. A tiny gasp came through her open lips. She jerked away from him, scurrying across the bed as if he were a spider.

"What are you doing in here?" she asked.

"My clothes were wet."

"What does that have to do with anything?"

"It was either stay in here or walk half naked into the salon for my duffel bag. I heard Travis and Haley talking out there."

She just looked at him.

"You were asleep by the time I dried off," he went on. "I was just going to lie here until Travis and Haley left the salon, but I fell asleep. I didn't mean to spend the whole night in here."

He climbed out of bed, giving her a view of his backside as he went into the bathroom. There was attraction and then there was this thing building between them. Attraction he could deal with. This he couldn't. Seeing the Arab man on top of her yesterday had brought out the animal in him. What if that man had killed her? The thought of losing her to another tragedy had cauterized him. It still did.

He'd lost his mother and his wife to tragedy, which hurt despite his wife's having wanted a divorce. That had been part of the tragedy. Knowing that she'd been unhappy with him and had died before she could find happiness had just about killed him.

Losing Farren would affect him in the same way and that had him worried. He'd promised himself a long time ago to be sure the next woman he got involved with could handle his profession, could handle him. Harder, tougher women than Farren. Women who didn't need a nine-to-five man.

That's why he stayed focused on military types. They'd

have more experience in dangerous situations and their emotions were less likely to be fragile. All he knew was he had to protect himself from facing the kind of loss he'd endured when Veronica died. His mother. He hadn't been able to save either woman. He'd tried with his mother, but he hadn't found a way to pull her from the depression that had gripped her ever since his dad died. The 9/11 tragedy had taken her from him before he could. A car accident had taken his wife before he could let her go the way she wanted.

What would falling for Farren do to him? He didn't trust her to have the staying power he needed from a woman. It wasn't her fault, it was just the way she was. He had to part ways with her before she mattered too much. Before she became yet another woman he failed. He hoped it wasn't already too late.

Emerging from the bathroom with a towel wrapped around his waist, he saw that Farren had pulled the covers to her chin and propped herself more upright against the pillows. Her big amber eyes watched him. He could almost hear her chattering away in her head.

There was this guy I knew once. We were friends, you know? Just friends. But one day we went to the park for a picnic and we found a grassy spot and after lunch I fell asleep and when I woke up I was curled next to him with my whole body touching his, you know, draped over his, really close, and, well, he got the wrong idea and...

Okay, maybe he was a little off in what she'd say, but it'd go something like that. He caught himself before he smiled, then left the cabin.

After dressing to fit the part of a yachter, Elam went up to the flybridge, where Travis and Keenan stood talking. They stopped when he appeared.

"Farren okay?" Travis asked.

"Yeah. Much better."

"Good. Because the congressman is having a cocktail party tonight. We think you and Farren should crash it," Keenan said.

Elam looked around. "Where is Haley?"

"She had a late night mingling with the other festival attendees. That's how she found out about the party."

"She didn't get back to the yacht until morning," Keenan answered. "I was on watch when she got here and told me." He glanced at Travis, making Elam do the same.

Travis didn't look pleased about Haley being out all night by herself.

"That's good. But I'll need a suit and Farren's going to need a dress."

"Haley said she had that under control. She brought something with her from the States."

"Really?"

"Yacht festival…nice clothes…the two kind of go hand-in-hand."

"What she lacks in her personal life she makes up for in her professional one."

Meaning, Haley knew how to dress nice but she didn't dress nice herself. Her past made it hard for Travis to deal with her on a personal level, because her personal life was still so unsteady. She hadn't been able to shed the horror of what had happened to her in Iraq. Travis had told him once that Haley had once enjoyed wearing feminine things when she wasn't working. Not anymore, not since Iraq.

"Is Farren going to be able to handle a cocktail party with you tonight?" Keenan asked.

The question yanked his attention to his own issues with women. One in particular. "She'll be fine."

A sound made him look with the other two toward the

stairs leading up to the flybridge and sundeck. Farren's hesitant glance moved from one man to the next until it landed on Elam and stayed a little longer as she passed. She wore a Hawaiian floral bathing suit with a pink sarong tied around her waist. A matching big pink straw hat shaded her eyes. She held an iPod in one hand, probably filled with every Avril Lavigne song ever produced.

Elam understood she was only playing a role, appearing on deck looking like a vacationer about to get some sun, but he still had to harden himself against the swell of affection circling his heart. Her ordeal had made her reach out to him, but that didn't change how different they were. She lived in an old farmhouse on a quiet island and he lived wherever his missions took him. Kids in the yard, barbecues with the neighbors, a kiss in the morning and an "I'll see you at dinner tonight" just weren't in his future. He couldn't give her that.

He watched her recline on the blue-and-white striped sunbathing pad. She kept her sarong on and pressed a button on the iPod.

Dread welled up in him right along with a good dose of desire. Seeing her dressed to the nines in a cocktail dress was going to drive him over the edge.

Farren let her held breath go as she walked into the salon. She'd stayed up on the sundeck long after Elam had left and hadn't seen him since.

"There you are," Haley said as she came out of the galley. Farren stopped as she approached.

"Mind if we go in your cabin for a minute?" Haley asked.

"What for?"

"I just need to talk to you about tonight."

"Tonight?"

"Didn't Elam tell you?"

"I haven't seen him since this morning."

Haley smiled. "Trying to avoid each other, huh?"

"What's happening tonight?" Farren resumed her walk to her cabin.

Haley followed. "A cocktail party."

"Whose?"

"Congressman Shay's."

Just inside the cabin, Farren stopped and faced Haley. "We were invited?"

"No. You're crashing it."

"Elam and I?"

"Yep." Haley smiled again.

"I don't have anything to wear. I didn't bring anything fancy."

"That's okay. Because I did." Haley gestured toward the bed.

Farren turned. And stared. Beige lining peeked through a mesh of beaded silk. In the middle, the bodice would dip nearly to her belly button and the triangular pieces that covered her breasts tapered to ridiculously thin spaghetti straps. The hem rose precariously high on one side and on the other side angled to a point just above the knee.

"Odie helped me with the size," Haley said.

Odie was a jack of all trades, apparently. What had she done, looked at a picture and known?

Farren went to the bed and lifted it for a closer look. "There's no way I can wear this." Her breasts would practically fall out of it. She felt funny about wearing something so sexy after what happened yesterday. But she had to admit, wearing it for Elam would be easy.

"Sorry. I didn't know you when I picked it out. I was

thinking fancy cocktail party on a yacht. I envisioned a different type of woman. Had I known…" Farren caught her giving her a thoughtful survey. "I would have bought something a little more…Cinderella." She smiled along with her teasing tone.

"I'll wear a sundress," Farren said, not sure if she should be insulted that a woman like Haley likened her to Cinderella, teasing or not. Then again, she shouldn't be surprised. Lots of people misjudged her. She dressed femininely and kept her nails meticulously groomed. People often had difficulty believing she was an electrical engineer.

"Not formal enough. You'll stand out too much."

"I don't mind."

"You'll look like you didn't come prepared. Like the decision to be here was impulsive."

"I didn't plan it."

"Think of the team, Farren. And Elam. We don't want anyone questioning his true purpose."

"I don't see the big deal. So what if Imaad knows. So what if Shay knows. Jared and Carolyn murdered each other and now a terrorist wants me to give him money."

"Imaad will disappear if he finds out who we are. If he finds out what kind of organization is after him."

"What kind of organization is that?"

"A secret one."

Farren tossed the dress onto the bed and went to the closet where she'd hung all her sundresses.

"A powerful one," Haley said. "TES has a reputation that even someone like Imaad wouldn't be able to ignore. He isn't safe in the shadows from an organization like ours. We can take him down without public, political consent. He would know that."

"He won't just turn away from three million."

"Of course not."

"But he would run from your organization? What are you, some kind of mafia with a cause?"

"No, nothing so theatrical. Our government would deny any involvement in a mission that resulted in the unauthorized killing of a rising terrorist figure, but who do you think is giving us our orders?"

Stunned, Farren slowly turned to face her. "You're saying Elam works for the government?"

"Not at all. He works in the gray area between that and the devil."

It sounded so risky. But brave and noble, too. *Heroic.* It fueled her feelings for him and confused her at the same time.

"Look," Haley said with a heavy sigh, "I'm probably telling you more than I should, but you're one of us now. You need to understand the importance of protecting this team. As long as our organization is protected, we can keep fighting terrorism without political ramifications. That's how you fight terrorism. You don't do it by waving at the camera and telling the American public how you're going to do your job. The job has to be secret." She paused but Farren didn't know what to say. She was still trying to wrap her mind around what she was learning.

"Wearing a sexy cocktail dress may seem insignificant," Haley continued, "but every little thing matters. One slip could lead to another and pretty soon people like Imaad are going to their leaders with questions. They find out how close they are to getting caught and disappear into caves. As an operative for TES, you go in, you get the job done, and you get out before anyone knows who you are."

"All right," Farren said. "I'll wear the dress."

Haley smiled. "Good girl." She headed for the door.

"You have two hours." At the door, she stopped, looking back. "Oh, and we didn't have this discussion."

Farren nodded. She caught the change in Haley's smile and wondered if she'd just been fooled into wearing a sexy dress for Elam. Except she didn't think Haley had lied to her about TES. Which touched her. And disturbed her.

Farren fingered the wisps of blond hair she'd left hanging free along her face and studied herself in the mirror. Softly lined brown eyes stared back at her and coral gloss shined on parted lips. She'd put her hair up and it made her neck look delicate and slender. The thin straps of the dress didn't seem like they'd hold the triangular strips of cloth that covered her breasts and dipped to her sternum. The skin-colored material under the black beaded silk netting made her look naked and that touched every curve of her body. The hem rode high on her left thigh and dipped to a point at her right knee. Too many hard angles for her taste, but she had to admit, it looked pretty darn good on her. She found a black onyx pendant to hang from a vintage-style chain and a pair of strappy black shoes that made her legs look long and slender.

She wondered what Elam would think. Anticipation gave her a rush. He'd like it. A lot. A shiver gave her shoulders a tiny jolt. Clutching a small black purse, she left the bathroom and went to the cabin door. There, she breathed in and exhaled. Opening the door, she walked down the hall.

She heard voices in the salon and stopped. Travis and Haley looked up and then Elam followed suit. She watched them all go still, but Elam most of all. His eyes flared with masculine interest. He made a stunning picture himself, tall and imposing in a black silk suit. The jacket made his shoulders look impossibly broad and fell straight over his flat stomach.

He'd combed his hair but it still looked messy, stylishly so, devilishly. He'd shaved, too, but there was still that rugged shadow, accentuating those sensuous lips.

She was the first to avert the connection, looking down at her ruby-red toes, curling then relaxing them.

Travis cleared his throat.

"Wow. You look beautiful," Haley said.

Farren raised her eyes, hearing the sincerity in her tone. She wondered if the woman ever wore dresses like this. Or any dresses for that matter.

"Looks like I didn't do too bad on that dress after all," Haley added.

"You should find a few of those for yourself," Travis said, earning himself a sidelong glare.

Elam smiled and moved toward Farren. He sauntered like a dark-haired Daniel Craig in a James Bond flick. He probably had a gun under that jacket, too.

"Let's go," he said, opening his elbow for her to hook her arm.

She slid her hand over his forearm and walked with him to the door. They separated as they climbed off the yacht, but once on the dock, she anchored to him again, the heels of her shoes too high for the lengthy walk to the congressman's boat. She felt sinewy muscle beneath his jacket and shirt and couldn't help looking down. His strong hand was relaxed in front of him, his thumb sloping to the curve of his long fingers. He'd saved her with those hands more than once. An image flashed of them touching her, running up her bare stomach from behind, rising higher. The occasional bump of their hips and brush of her breasts against his biceps added to the fantasy.

"I heard this story once," she said, and he turned with a grin. She ignored his wry expectancy of the chatter that would follow. "It was about a girl that worked at the same company where I used to work. She was a janitor, so I'd see her every once in a while. Everyone talked about her. She had this bleached-blond hair with a pink streak and wore this dark eyeliner and bright blue eye shadow and bright lipstick. But it was the way she dressed that got my attention, and everyone else's. She always wore skirts. Mostly jean skirts, but they were always short, above the knee, and with that she'd wear tight T-shirts or tank tops with some weird bright-colored shirt over it. She looked like a rock star.

"Anyway, somebody told me she lived with a guy who had five DUIs and had been to prison once and who couldn't hold a job. He was a mechanic and had piercings and tattoos and green spiked hair. The girl grew up without a dad and her mother was a meth addict and couldn't take care of her. That's how she ended up living with the guy.

"I used to think she looked so out of place the way she dressed. She had such pretty features and this petite little body. It was like she was fragile trying to appear tough."

"Okay, I give up. What's the point of that story?" he asked.

"There is no point."

"There's always a point."

Really? She eyed him, searching his profile for signs of teasing. There were none. He was busy watching their surroundings.

"I didn't mean for there to be a point," she said.

He glanced at her, his gaze falling over her body. "Do you feel out of place in that dress?"

"Well…" She looked down at the front of her, at the illusion of bare skin beneath the mesh of beaded silk. "Yeah, but…"

He chuckled and resumed his proficient watchfulness. "It's scary how well I'm getting to know you."

"You don't know me that well."

"I know you start talking when you're nervous or uncomfortable. But there's usually a point."

"You think the point of that story is I feel uncomfortable in this dress?"

"No. I think the point is you feel like that girl right now. You think you look good but people would have to look deeper to see it's not the real you."

She smiled. "That's awfully sensitive and insightful of you, Elam. Does this mean you're in touch with your feminine side?"

He shook his head. "Like I said, scary."

She laughed lightly. "Who would have thought?"

"It's just an observation."

Anyone looking at him now would never know he was uncomfortable. He exuded such confidence and his physical form was so imposing. But she knew he was uncomfortable. "An endearing one."

He didn't acknowledge her, but she wasn't ready to abandon this topic. "Want me to tell you something I know about you?"

"I'm not sure. Do I?" He sounded wary but game for playing along.

"You always have to be in control. I think that's the real reason you do what you do." Okay, so this was a lot more serious than he'd made it, but she couldn't resist.

"What do you mean?"

"Like now. The way you keep watching around us. As if you need to be ready for anything that jumps out at us."

"I do."

"Yeah, but you never let your feelings get away from you."

"Farren—"

"Wait. Let me finish. When you're on an assignment, you have to be in control. Loss of control could mean a mistake and that could mean your life or the life of one of your teammates. And since you're always on assignment somewhere, you never have to face losing control of your emotions in a relationship. I'm sure relationships don't even have a chance to develop into something that would threaten you that way."

"Is this some kind of therapy session? I thought you were an engineer."

She ignored his defensive tone. It only confirmed she was right.

"I've seen you lose control." At the bazaar when she'd seen him through the rear window of her abductors' car. He'd been frightened. The stoic TES operative had lost his focus, his certainty. She'd seen the same after he'd saved her—the urgency on his face, the worry. Fear.

He stopped and faced her. "You like it when I lose control?"

"It's not that. It's just an observation," she echoed his words, and watched the tension ease a little from around his eyes.

"You should do that more often," she said, smiling.

"Lose control?"

"Some things you just can't control, Elam. Recognize that. Accept it. Let whatever is holding you back go." Meaning his tragic past.

He stared into her eyes, directly and powerfully. Nothing intimidated this man. Yet her assessment had triggered his defenses.

"I can't stop doing what I do," he finally said.

"You don't have to deny yourself things you need and want in order to fight for a good cause."

"I realize that."

"I don't think you do."

His eyes narrowed a fraction.

"Not every woman would feel the way your wife did."

"Are you saying you don't?" he challenged.

Their conversation came to a halt as they approached the congressman's yacht. People stood on every visible deck and music filtered through the air. She didn't know how she felt. She thought she knew, but now she wasn't sure. What would it be like to be with a man like Elam?

She turned and met his now very cynical gaze. Once again, she'd confirmed his theory. Her silence and uncertainty spoke for her. And his emotions would remain closed until he saw how narrow his view was. It didn't have to be a military woman who matched him. It could be anyone who loved him.

"Come on." He put his hand on her lower back and guided her toward the yacht. "Let's get this over with."

Chapter 9

Let's get this over with.

Farren stepped inside the elegant yacht, pondering the emotion behind that statement. Elam's irritation convinced her she'd nailed the truth. But what did she want to do with it? Have sex with him? Would it mean too much? What if he was right for her? What if, for the first time ever, she'd gotten it right?

She glanced over at him. His face was a mask now. He searched the crowd on the yacht, all business, all mission. The soft tones of a piano wafted through the air. Women in long and short, sparkly and smooth cocktail gowns mingled among men in dark suits. Some held champagne flutes. Some held cocktail glasses. One man held a bottle of beer.

"Excuse me."

Farren turned with Elam to see a security guard behind them.

"I don't believe you were invited."

"We were just passing by," Elam said.

The security guard's gaze drifted over them both in disdain. "I'm afraid I'm going to have to ask you to leave."

"Why, Elam and Farren," a staged feminine voice cooed. "How good of you to come." Farren saw Bev approach, glass of champagne in hand. "Go away, Edward. I told them they could come." She shooed the man with her hand.

Edward hesitated but finally wandered off.

Bev leaned closer to Farren and said in a low voice, "He's a pushover for a security guard. I met him at the door."

Farren smiled. "Is that why he believed you? You lie so well."

Bev laughed. "No one will care. It's nothing."

If only she knew. Farren glanced over the crowd, looking for Congressman Shay.

"How did you manage to get an invitation?" Elam asked Bev.

"I didn't." She laughed again. "Like you, I invited myself." She turned and saw the redhead, Sara. With a wave, she glided off. "I'll catch up to you two later."

Farren caught sight of Shay through the crowd. He stood next to Edward, who must have just finished telling him they were here. Shay looked at her with a grim set to his jaw. A tall brunette passed her and Elam, sending Elam a flirtatious glance. Her neckline rivaled Farren's and did a fine job of catching his attention.

She elbowed him. He looked at her, then in the direction she indicated.

Shay started toward them. Was it her imagination, or was he more interested in her than Elam? Maybe that wasn't surprising, since it was her mother who wrote the name of his yacht on her itinerary.

"I'd say welcome aboard, but I'm not sure if I should," Shay said to Elam.

"We heard about your party and couldn't stay away. The rave of the marina and all."

"I'm sure." He turned to Farren. "Ms. Gage, you look radiant."

"Thank you." She resisted the urge to cover her cleavage.

"I trust you are enjoying Marmaris while you're here?" he asked. Then to Elam, "I hope it isn't just business that brought you here."

"We're getting around," Elam said. "In fact, just yesterday Farren was accosted outside the bazaar by some of Imaad's men."

Though he was using it to goad Shay, the reminder of how close she'd come to being raped dimmed her mood.

Shay's eyes sobered and he looked at her. "Accosted? What happened?"

"Nothing," she said, too quickly. She didn't feel like talking about it. She sent Elam a narrow look. He ignored her.

"She left the bazaar ahead of me and some of Imaad's men forced her into a car."

"They kidnapped you?" He sounded outraged.

"Elam was never far behind," she said.

Shay moved his gaze to Elam, silently comprehending what must have taken place. "Why did they do it?"

"I bet you could explain that better than me."

With a frustrated smirk, he turned to Farren. He studied her closely. "You look all right...are you?"

She nodded, wondering if he actually cared.

"What did they want? Do you know?"

She didn't think she misread the concern she heard.

"Imaad al Rasoon is threatening her for three million," Elam said for her. "But you probably already know that."

The congressman only sent him an impatient glance but his attention came back to Farren. "I didn't know."

"I wonder."

"Ms. Gage, I fail to see how you think I can help you."

"Spoken like a true politician," she retorted, not believing for a second that he was being straight with them.

"What do you know about Imaad?" Elam asked.

"What makes you think I know anything?"

"You make it a priority to know all terrorists who pose a threat to honest, God-loving Catholics."

Shay let out a long breath. "I don't know much. But I do know he's spent some time expanding a camp along Turkey's border with Iraq. He's one to watch, if not more." The pointed look he sent Elam made Farren wonder what he meant by more.

"Could Carolyn have discovered her husband's dealings with him?" Elam asked, not appearing to have noticed the look, though she didn't doubt he had. Elam had a way of appearing oblivious even though his mind never stopped working.

Shay nodded. "If her husband was dealing with him, I suppose it's possible."

"Would she have had a reason to come to you for help?" Farren asked.

This time the congressman couldn't hide his reaction. Not completely. Farren caught the fleeting look of regret in his eyes before he covered it.

"I wouldn't know the answer to that."

"I think you do," Farren said. "What are you hiding, Mr. Shay? And why?"

He didn't respond right away. But finally he said, "I worry about your safety, Ms. Gage, but I don't think I can do any better than Mr. Rhule, here, in helping you." He looked directly at Elam. "Your background with the army is quite impressive."

"Did some reading, I see." Elam didn't seem the least bit ruffled.

"I found it particularly interesting that your career seems to have suddenly ended about two years ago. You didn't retire and you didn't go to work for anyone else…at least…not overtly."

"I don't share my resume with just anyone."

The congressman's sly smile said he wasn't falling for it. "With good reason, I'm sure."

Just then, his wife appeared at his side, sliding her gaze from Farren, to Elam, to Shay. "Is everything all right?"

Shay's smile smoothed. "Fine, darling."

Facing Elam and Farren again, he swept his arm to his left, indicating the table full of appetizers. "Please, make yourselves comfortable. I should attend to my other guests."

Farren sent him a look that would let him know she wasn't fooled.

The congressman guided his wife away with him.

"Now we know what's keeping him from talking," Farren said. "His wife."

"It sure seems that way."

"You think there's more?"

"He's afraid of something."

"Like his wife finding out he was having an affair?"

"Maybe. But that doesn't explain why Carolyn would come all the way to Turkey to be with him." Taking her hand in his, he led her up the stairs to the sundeck and then to the aft rail, away from the handful of other people mingling there.

She leaned her backside against the rail. Boat lights sparkled everywhere in the marina. It was a beautiful, still night. He stood before her. For a second she got lost in the pool-water blue of his eyes.

"I still think my mother was afraid of Jared and that's why she came to Bodrum," Farren said.

"It's looking more and more that way. If she knew about his deal with Imaad, she had plenty of reason to be afraid. But why come all the way to Bodrum?"

"It's far away. And Turkey is the last place he'd expect her to go."

"Especially if she knew Imaad was here."

"Jared probably knew, too. All she had to do was make it to Marmaris. If they were lovers, Shay would have protected her once she got here even if he didn't know she was coming."

"She could have gone to a hotel in Marmaris if that's all she wanted."

"Jared could've found her a lot easier that way. A hotel would've placed her somewhere. In a yacht, she would've been mobile. And since she flew into Bodrum, he wouldn't have known she planned to go to Marmaris. Maybe Shay was going to help her disappear."

His eyebrows rose in consideration and he nodded with a slight smile. "You're pretty good at this."

She gave him a feigned coy look. "And I'm not even military."

"You'd have all the men tripping over themselves if you were. Trying to protect you instead of doing their duty."

"Just because I like dresses doesn't mean I can't take care of myself."

"Doesn't matter. Men are instinctively protective creatures when it comes to the softer sex."

She laughed as he took her hand and tugged her off the rail to sweep her into a dance. Sliding her arm over his shoulder, she moved with him to a Frank Sinatra song. "This Town." She could see just over his shoulder. A couple sat at the bar, forward and toward the flybridge. Another sat at a small table near there. It seemed this was the place to go for quiet time alone. Time alone with him.

Farren let herself enjoy the dance. But she was very aware of his hand on the small of her back, holding her close as they moved.

"I always liked Sinatra," he said.

She dipped her head back a little more so she wouldn't have to strain her eyes so much to see him. "A big tough guy like you listens to Frank Sinatra?"

He just grinned down at her.

"Oh…wait a minute," she teased. "You mean you actually *like* something?"

"I told you I like lots of things."

"You never mentioned anything specific."

"It never came up until now."

They were beginning to sound like a couple who'd just started dating. She stopped smiling so dreamily up at him. It was too easy to like him. He saw the change in her and the silly infatuation left his face, too. He stopped dancing and so did she.

"Would the two of you like something to drink?"

Farren turned with Elam to see Shay behind the white-topped bar. The couple who'd been sitting on the black stools were gone, but the other still sat at the table, leaning close and absorbed in conversation.

Elam released her and she walked to one of the bar stools, too curious not to take him up on his invitation. What had changed his mind? Why did he now want to talk to them?

She sat on a stool. The hem of her dress exposed her

thigh almost to her underwear. She saw Elam notice and her heart skipped a few beats. He stopped beside her, not taking a stool. His gaze devoured her leg for what seemed like minutes but was probably more like a few seconds, then it roved up her body until he reached her eyes.

"Club soda for me," Farren said, turning to Shay.

"Nothing for me," Elam said.

Shay's smile turned sage as he prepared the drink. "If I didn't know better, I'd think you two knew each other before now." He slid the glass of club soda over to Farren.

"How do you know we didn't know each other before now?" Elam asked.

"I just know."

"We met in Bodrum," Farren said.

"By coincidence?"

"Something like that."

He studied her, speculating. "It's interesting that you both chose Bodrum to vacation and just happened to be there at the same time." He moved his gaze to Elam. "You, an expert marksman who doesn't share his resume, and an electrical engineer from a reclusive island in Maine who's just inherited millions."

He'd done a lot of checking since their first meeting. Was he debating whether or not to talk to them? Would answering his questions help? She looked at Elam.

"I could hardly believe it myself," he quipped.

Shay didn't seem to appreciate the humor. He turned to Farren again. "However you met, it's good you did."

She wasn't so sure about that. "What makes you say that?"

"You don't strike me as someone who has much experience with nefarious characters."

She couldn't help glancing at Elam, whose hint of a grin told her enough.

"It's both incredible and curious that your mother left you her fortune. When did she abandon you?"

The unexpected way he asked sharpened her awareness. "When I was four. Why?"

"She never contacted you after that?"

"No." Why was he asking?

His brow creased above his nose. "Did you ever try to locate her?"

She supposed it wouldn't hurt to indulge his curiosity. Maybe it would lead to information that could help them. "I asked my foster parents about her, but they didn't know anything. So of course, I didn't find her. She didn't want me to find her."

"I can't imagine how a mother could abandon her child."

She didn't comment. There was nothing to say. Nothing would change what already was and she didn't understand it, either. But she wondered about the emotion she thought she heard in his voice.

"How old are you now?" he asked.

Why did he ask such a question? She began to feel tense. "Thirty-one."

"Did she ever send you anything? Christmas or birthday presents?"

"No. I had no contact with her whatsoever."

He hesitated. "When is your birthday?"

"Excuse me?"

"Your birthday. When is it?"

He wanted to know the date? "June fourteenth."

She watched him calculate the years and months, keeping his gaze steady. A chill raced down her spine and arms. Why was her birthday important? Another chill raced through her. Did he wonder if he was her father?

"How did you know my mother?" she demanded. His

questions were too focused not to have a purpose. How many times as a child had she dreamed of her real father driving up and whisking her away from her loveless life? Only this wasn't the way she'd dreamed it. This felt wrong. Off.

Someone came up the stairs before he answered. Maybe he never intended to answer. Shay's wife stepped up to the sundeck and smiled when she saw her husband. But Farren could tell it was staged. She was watching him. As if she didn't trust him.

"You're always sneaking away from me," she said, moving to the bar. "Maybe you should introduce me to your new friends."

"Elam, Farren, my wife, Pauline."

"Is there something specific you came to talk to my husband about?"

"No. We heard he was here and wanted to say hello," Elam said.

Farren watched the congressman, who hid his relief.

"If you'll excuse us." Shay headed for the stairs. His wife hesitated, eyeing Elam and Farren before she followed.

Crossing her legs, Farren looked up at Elam. "That was interesting."

"Which, his wanting to know your birthday or the way his wife keeps track of him?" His eyes lifted from looking at her crossed legs.

She uncrossed her legs and got off the bar stool. She was so confused right now. The feeling that the congressman had asked about her birthday for a reason disturbed her. That reason awakened an old, deep longing she hadn't thought still occupied the hidden recesses of her heart. Elam's constant presence and heated attention only added to her disarray.

"We can probably go now," she said. "He isn't going to

talk to us any more tonight." Not wanting him to notice how frazzled she was, she turned and started down the stairs.

Elam caught up to her in the hall leading to the salon. "Hey." He grasped her hand and stopped her. "What's the matter?"

She shook her head and was on the verge of tears. This was an absurd time to cry. Why cry? What was there to cry about? Shay?

Elam held her chin in his hand, keeping her from lowering her head like she wanted. Moisture stung her eyes.

"If he had an affair with her..."

"If he did it happened recently," Elam said.

Recently. Yes. Who had affairs that lasted thirty-one years? "What if they got back together after..." She couldn't finish.

"He only asked when your birthday was. He was curious about Carolyn leaving her daughter."

"Yeah." She felt like she was hyperventilating.

He moved his hand alongside her neck, his thumbs brushing her jaw. "It's okay. Breathe slower."

She focused on his eyes and tried to do what he said. It didn't work.

"Okay?" he said in a raspy voice.

The sound worked better than anything. He grounded her. How did he do that? She started to catch her breath, only to lose it again as she drowned in his eyes.

He stepped toward her. In the narrow hall it didn't take much to crowd her against the wall. He angled his head and kissed her. She opened her mouth and took him in.

Voices carried from the salon, but the hall curved and hid them from view. Only people on their way to the sundeck would pass this way, and since the sun was no longer shining, most everyone was either in the salon and dining area or on the aft deck. But all that drifted out of her consciousness as he moved his mouth with hers. Her pulse took flight along with her escalating desire. If he was doing this to distract her, it was working.

He moved his hand down her body. He sizzled a path around her bare thigh, sending tongues of flame shooting up her leg. She lifted her knee to his hip and struggled to catch her breath as his hand ran up the length of her thigh and slid around to the bare skin her thong didn't cover. She could feel his erection against her.

He kissed her harder. Sensation consumed her. *Yes. She needed this. Him.* Let it take her away from the implications of Shay's curiosity. He could take her somewhere beautiful. She immersed herself in him and what he made her feel. Let them take her. These feelings he strummed to life.

Parting his jacket, she slid her hands over him, over the straps of his gun holster. It made her hotter. She leaned to kiss his neck. Ran her tongue over his skin. She wanted him so much. Needed him.

She dragged her hand down over his hard chest and stomach, her fingers catching on the straps of his gun holster. When she found the silky material of his trousers, she curled her fingers around his hard length. She tipped her head back and closed her eyes, the fantasy of him sliding inside her too powerful.

He hissed a curse, dampening her skin with his tongue as he blazed a trail down her neck. She used both hands to unfasten his trousers. All he'd have to do is move her underwear out of the way.

A low growl rumbled inside him, a strangled sound.

"Do me," she said. "Now."

"Farren." He slid his hand off her bare rear and took hold of hers.

She lowered her leg from its perch on his hip and let her forehead rest against his chin. "Don't stop." But she knew he had to. They were in a bad place for this, and she was still reeling from the revelations that had come from their conversation with Shay.

She didn't want to think about all the years she'd spent dreaming of a real father she'd never met. Congressman Shay had come out of nowhere. He'd blindsided her. She hadn't seen this coming. But she couldn't escape it. Not here, anyway.

"I don't have any condoms," Elam said.

Leaning against the opposite wall, he stared at her. He didn't have any condoms, but she wanted to take him back to *Rapture* and let him make love to her. And she knew that's what would happen. If she let him. She wanted to.

What was she thinking?

Pushing off the wall, she hurried into the salon. She meant to go straight to the door, but Shay stood next to his wife, talking to another man close to his age. He saw her and she stopped, unable to keep herself from staring. His age made it hard to see any signs of resemblance. She couldn't believe she was even making the assessment. But then she noticed the way he looked at her. Was it regret she saw in his eyes? Worry? What could he be worried about? Exposure?

Elam hooked her arm with his and steered her to the door. She was grateful to him for helping her. Her mind was such a mass of churning confusion she didn't know what to do with it.

Outside on the dock, she kept her arm linked with Elam's as they walked. All the way back to *Rapture*, she ran and reran in her mind how it could be possible. How it couldn't. She didn't want it to be possible. Not someone like Shay, someone who could be connected to the threats she'd been getting. What did he know? And if she was his daughter, how long had he known? Would he let Imaad kill her to protect his secrets? *His own daughter? Was she his daughter?* It all made her sick.

She left Elam's support as they approached the yacht. Stepping aboard, she didn't stop until she was in her cabin.

"He just asked about your birthday," Elam said.

And she realized he'd followed her in here. The door was closed.

"Shouldn't you be briefing your team?" she asked.

"That can wait until morning." He loosened his tie and then shrugged out of his jacket, draping it over the arm of the chair by the bed. She hugged her arms at the sight of him in black suit pants and a white dress shirt with the black straps of his gun holster over his shoulders.

"Just because he asked about your birthday doesn't mean he's your father."

"I don't want to talk about this."

"And even if he had an affair with her back then and resumed it now, it still doesn't mean he's your father."

"Don't." She put her hands to her ears and turned her back. She didn't want to hope, only to have that hope crushed in the end. Besides, if Congressman Shay was her father, he hadn't wanted her any more than her mother had.

Elam's hands slid around her sides and he wrapped her in his arms. She lowered hers, putting her hands over his, startled that he'd come so close.

"I'm sorry," he said, and she knew he didn't mean just for talking about it. He was sorry that what they may have discovered upset her.

Staying close, she turned, putting h.. .. ..ds on his chest and looking up at his face. He made her feel so good. His arms looped comfortably around her. He watched her warily, as if trying to gauge where this was headed. She rose onto her toes and pressed a kiss to his lips. She wasn't going to fight it anymore.

He didn't move. A shiver of pleasure rushed through her senses. She pressed another kiss to his warm, soft lips, opening her eyes to see his shadowed and full of growing lust.

She put her mouth on his once again, this time staying there, moving her lips, adjusting, then taking him deeper. He gave her his tongue and he took over the kiss. She let him have her. His unsteady breath ran through her like a strand of music. She folded her arms over his shoulders to bring herself against him as close as she could be. The hard angles of his gun and holster dug into her skin. His hands moved over her back. One stopped midway down her back, the other lower. He tightened his hold, stealing her breath.

Then he eased away, lifting his mouth out of her reach and sliding his hands to her waist. She lowered from her toes and looked up at him.

"We can't do this," he said.

And her spirits deflated. He was shutting her out again. Last time he blamed three glasses of wine. What would it be now?

"Why not?"

"I don't have any protection." He moved away, going toward the chair.

That was the only reason?

He sat on the chair and removed his shoes, keeping his eyes trained on her. She walked toward him. Alertness intensified the hunger in his eyes. He dropped his socks and leaned back in the chair, barefoot, tie askew, still wearing his holster.

God, why did that turn her on so much? She was feeling reckless enough not to care. And she was tired of waiting for things to go her way. It was time to start taking what she wanted. And right now, she wanted him.

Hiking up the jagged hem of her dress, she straddled him. He put his hands on her waist, his thumbs firm on her abdomen. Running her hands up his chest, she leaned over his mouth.

"I don't want you to use a condom," she whispered, and reveled in the way his eyes flinched ever so slightly with responding heat. "I want to feel you naked inside me."

She put her mouth on his, then moved along his jaw, breathing in the smell of man, listening to his barely audible curse. She smiled and kissed his throat. She ran her tongue over his skin until she reached his ear. "What are you going to do about that?" she whispered some more.

But she didn't wait for an answer. She tugged at his tie until it came undone, moving back to pull it from around his neck, watching his face as she did it. His jaw flexed. His eyes fired with tenuous control over his passion. She tossed the tie over her shoulder.

Reaching for his collar, she unbuttoned it and kept going down the front of his shirt. When she arrived at his pants, she stopped to spread her hands on his bare skin. She felt his muscles jerk with tension.

"Oh," she sighed long and languorous. It felt better than she ever imagined.

She felt her way from his abdomen to his chest, thumbing his nipples and leaning forward to kiss him. He kissed her back, and that was all the initiating she had to do. His fingers removed the clip holding her hair up. Bobby pins fell to the floor as he ran his fingers through the strands. She pulled the tiny straps off her shoulders, kept drawing them down until she freed her arms and the front of the dress slumped. He joined her effort and tugged the dress down, exposing her breasts. Holding them in his hands, he leaned forward and took what he could of one in his mouth.

She put her hands over the round balls of his biceps and watched him move to the other breast. The sensation became unbearable. She needed more. Dipping her head, she kissed his temple. He lifted his head and gave her his mouth. While he kissed her, he unfastened his trousers, breaking away from her mouth to shove them down his legs.

Rising up onto her knees to accommodate, she pulled the hem of her dress up, her long blond hair falling in front of one of her eyes. She tossed her hair out of the way and inched back over him on her knees.

"Are you on the Pill?"

She guided him with her hand. The tip of him entered. "No."

He stiffened underneath her, but she let her weight fall and felt him impale her all the way.

"Farren," he gritted from between his teeth.

She moved her hips. "I want this."

He swore.

Taking his face between her hands, sensing his cooling passion, she kissed him. "I want this," she said again.

His eyes linked with hers in a long and meaningful, telling moment. He was almost as gone as her. *Almost.*

She rose up on her knees, making him slide out until only the tip of him remained inside. Then she came back down, bringing her mouth and tongue to his while sweet, sweet friction changed strands of music to a roar in her head.

"Mmm…" He took hold of her hips in a mindless grip and began pumping his hips.

She put her hands on his shoulders for better leverage. His hands on her hips felt erotic. She was beginning to love his hands. His artful moves kept the roar going strong inside her, until it consumed her. Her pulse throbbed in her temples. Feeling engulfed her. It mushroomed into something she could no longer comprehend. Maybe she never had. What she felt for him. Elam. His essence entwined with hers. Her release came, relentless and tearing, leaving her trembling and weak.

She collapsed against him, feeling and hearing his own climax die on a guttural moan.

He didn't move at first. Just held her while their breathing evened.

She hoped he wasn't going to start talking now. He didn't. Just pulled her higher onto his hips and held her as he stood. She wrapped her legs around him until he brought her to the bed, where he planted her to sit. He stepped back and finished removing his clothes, putting the gun and holster on the chair. She lifted the dress off her, only then realizing that her strappy black shoes had fallen off sometime during their lovemaking.

Crawling under the covers, she watched him walk naked to the other side and get in beside her. She lay on her back, uncertain what he was thinking.

"Come here," he said, and a flood of warmth washed through her. She rolled to her side and moved closer. He held his arm open for her. She caught the softness of his eyes before she lay against him with a satisfied sigh. Maybe, just maybe, they had a chance.

Chapter 10

Elam kissed the corner of her mouth. The soft touches sent tingles across her skin. Smiling, she opened her eyes, sleepy and content.

"You didn't think we were finished, did you?" he asked in a gruff, bedroom voice.

"Did I give you that impression?" she teased right back.

He chuckled. "Not at all." And rolled on top of her.

Light from the marina filtered through the open drapes of the small window. Otherwise it was dark, casting Elam's face and shoulders in deep shadows. His blue eyes glowed as he gazed down into her eyes.

She ran her hands up his sides and around to his chest, where she tested the hard flesh before hooking her arms around his neck. His mouth curved in a slight smile, making his eyes crinkle at the corners. It bubbled up a lighthearted and soft laugh of her own.

He pushed one of her legs aside with his knee, making room for both of his. She hooked her ankles over his butt. He grunted when that movement pressed him against her. She stopped smiling when he ground his erection where she still ached for him.

Drawing in a much-needed breath of air, she dug her head back into the mattress and closed her eyes, giving in to sensation.

"You're so amazing." He took her lips with his for a messy, hot kiss. "Beautiful."

She sought more of his mouth. More connection. More everything. His fingers dug into her hair and he gave her what she wanted. His other hand moved from her rear up her side, lighting a ball of fire low in her abdomen that radiated all the way to her heart. He lifted his head, and his gaze melted into hers as he found his way to her waiting heat.

An involuntary sound of pleasure escaped from her. He drank it from her lips and tongue. She felt dizzy with feeling.

He pushed into her inch by slow inch. She blinked her eyes open. His looked right into hers, leaving nothing from her. No emotion. No vulnerability. The intensity of it stole her soul. She shuddered.

"Elam."

Oh, God, this meant too much.

Just as panic began to swell, he buried himself deep inside her and withdrew with deliberate slowness. He made love to her like that, holding her gaze with his, driving her panic away. He captured her heart and claimed it, making her irrevocably his.

Farren woke through a groggy fog. Moaning, she rolled from her side to her back, her hand plopping down on the pillow above her head. A few moments later, she came up onto her elbows and realized Elam wasn't in the cabin.

Disappointment ruined her morning bliss. She checked the clock affixed to the night table. Almost one. No longer morning.

Maybe that was why he wasn't here.

She rolled out of bed and went to shower. All the while an increasing unease encroached upon her. *What did last night mean? More important, what did it mean to Elam?* She was afraid to look too closely at what it meant to her. A lot. Exactly what she had feared. She'd leave it at that.

She shut off the shower. Dried herself. Dressed.

By the time she put her hand on the doorknob to leave the cabin, dread consumed her. She didn't want to see Elam's face. What if he distanced himself from her now?

Her heart beat faster and a fine tremble gave her shoulders a shiver and made her hands unsteady. She tried not to dwell on memories of last night and to focus instead on what had led to what had happened. The discovery that Shay could be her father had left her vulnerable and searching for answers she'd likely never get. Just like when she was a child. The old feelings Shay had dredged to the surface had thrown her—made her wish, even now, that she could know what it was to be part of a real family. That vulnerability had led to what happened with Elam. He had served as an outlet. But that outlet meant more to her than an affair.

She was doing it again. Desperation was what made her crawl onto Elam's lap. That deep-seated need of hers to feel wanted. She couldn't escape the foundation of her childhood. No matter how hard she tried, she couldn't outgrow the insecurities. Couldn't overrule them through sheer will.

So what would it take? Real love? Wasn't that what she'd felt last night?

She jerked her hand away from the doorknob. But it turned anyway, slowly, quietly. The door inched open and there stood Elam, stopping short when he saw her.

He didn't smile or say anything. She sensed his awkwardness. Or was it guardedness? She felt him assess her. The morning after…

How did he feel about it? Did he want to explore it further or would he rather distance himself in preparation for the day they went their separate ways?

Flustered, she pushed the door open wider and brushed past him. No one was in the salon. She came around the wall and entered the dining area and galley. Haley looked up from a plate of salad, a laptop open and running beside it.

"Sleeping Beauty wakes at last," she commented with a laugh.

Farren ignored her and zeroed in on the coffeemaker.

"Must have been some party." Haley did a poor job of hiding her speculation. "Elam was just in here. He brewed a fresh pot of coffee. I think he went back into your room to get his gun."

There was a bag of bagels on the counter. Farren shot Haley an unappreciative frown before grabbing one and pouring herself a cup of coffee. When she turned toward the table, Elam entered the galley, shrugging into a short-sleeved button-down shirt that covered the holster he now wore. The reminder that he was armed, just as the rest of the crew was, worked to push her discomfort away. Imaad was still out there, watching and waiting for the right time to pounce.

She made the mistake of looking at his eyes, which were intent and right on her. He seemed angry about something. Did he think she felt as though she'd settled for less than her ideals? She wouldn't call it settling, but she still didn't trust him to be there for her after they returned to

the States. He was too devoted to his job and too convinced any woman like his former wife wouldn't work for
him, wouldn't accept him the way he was. Truth was, she
couldn't reassure him. Her idea of a family man wasn't a
sniper who'd be gone a lot on dangerous missions.

Sitting at one end of the table, she broke a piece of bagel
off and put it in her mouth. Elam poured a cup of coffee and
brought a bagel to the table. He sat at the opposite end. Farren
slowed her chewing, nerves rolling in her stomach. She sipped
some coffee and couldn't stop her eyes from looking at him.

Those eyes dissected her. She had no doubt of his anger
now. He didn't like her withdrawal.

Well, what did he expect? She couldn't keep throwing
herself at him. Not when he'd in all likelihood end up no different from every other man she thought was worth the risk.

Haley's eyes rolled right and left, checking both ends
of the table as she ate her salad.

Travis and Keenan walked into the galley.

"Good, you're both up," Travis said. "What happened
last night?"

A shock wave hit Farren and she looked at Elam.

"Shay wouldn't talk," he said, keeping his eyes on her.

Keenan retrieved a bottle of water out of the refrigerator. "He isn't going to, then." He twisted the cap off the
bottle and drank.

"An affair with a woman whose husband is an arms
dealer would destroy his career," Travis said.

"Maybe he wasn't having an affair. Maybe his anti-
terrorism angle is all an act," Haley said. "He might have
been in on the deal."

"And Carolyn was working with her husband?" Keenan
drained the water bottle.

Haley nodded.

"Then why is Imaad here?" Travis asked. "He planned to come here before he knew Farren was going to be here, remember."

"Maybe not," Elam interjected. "Ameen chartered the *Sea Minstrel* after Farren arrived in Bodrum."

"But you said Asil had a Marmaris Yacht Festival brochure near his body."

Elam nodded. "That's right. So Imaad was planning to be in Marmaris before Farren came to Bodrum. What does that tell us?"

"That Congressman Shay is the key," Haley answered. "He's what's linking it all together."

Farren watched all four of them mull that over for a moment.

"Maybe we should just take Imaad out," Travis said. "Elam, you could get a clear shot from here."

"I think we should wait until we know what Shay's involvement is," Haley said.

"I agree," Keenan said.

"Me, too," Elam said, "although putting a hole in Imaad's forehead would put an end to this."

"We'll get Shay to talk," Haley said. "We just need a little more time."

"All right," Travis said. "I'll be on deck. Imaad's men have been wandering the docks all morning. We need to keep an eye on them."

Haley put her fork down and stood. "I'll go with you."

"Maybe I'll take a stroll on the pier," Keenan said.

Elam didn't move from his seat. Farren looked down at her bagel and lost her appetite.

"You're awfully quiet," he commented.

Farren heard the edge in his voice. She looked up at him and shrugged. "I didn't want to interrupt."

A moment passed before he said, "Is something wrong?"

"No."

"You normally talk more."

"I'm fine."

"I don't believe you."

"Why? Because I'm not talking everyone's ears off?"

He angled his head. "Maybe I missed something. I thought your climbing on my lap meant you liked me."

"What?"

"You heard me."

She stared at him. Was he angry at himself for falling for a woman he thought was wrong for him? Or did he just want to know why she'd withdrawn? Well, all right. She'd let him know.

"I didn't settle," she said. She didn't land Mr. Average and Full of Commitment, either. But she kept that to herself. She didn't land him, period.

Long seconds passed. Farren watched his emotion begin to soften. For some reason that piqued her.

"Will that make you feel better when this is over and you go your own way?" she asked.

He angled his head and eyed her derisively.

"Well?" she pushed him.

He straightened his head and met her gaze dead-on. "We didn't use a condom."

Was he insinuating that if she was pregnant they'd see each other again? She didn't want such obligation. All the reasons she didn't want to get involved with him reared up in her head. *Never home. Sniper. But those hands...*

Oh, God, how could she love them so much? They were killing hands, yet they were capable of gentle caresses. Gentle, intoxicating caresses.

"You didn't get me pregnant."

"What if it ends up that I do?"

"What would you do if it did?"

His jaw clenched and relaxed. "I'd do what's right."

"What? Marry me?"

When he didn't answer, she knew that's not what he really wanted.

"I'm not pregnant." She sure as hell hoped not, anyway. The timing should be wrong, but…who knew? She fisted her hand in her lap. Damn it, how could she have allowed herself to be so careless? She'd never done anything like that before. She'd never slept with a man and not seen to her protection. That had always been important. Except with Elam, it had been more important to feel him inside her.

"Would you tell me?"

His question snapped her back into focus. She searched his eyes. Slowly, she nodded, more confused than ever. He'd never answered her question about whether they'd see each other when this was over. His only concern was whether or not he'd gotten her pregnant.

That could only mean his heart was still shut tight to outsiders. He wouldn't risk another loss in his life. Unless a child were involved. What kind of father would that make him?

A responsible one.

Unfortunately, Farren wanted more than that in her man. She wanted his heart, too. Even if his job kept him away from home a lot, if she had his heart, she could make it work. It was the only way it *would* work. Didn't he see that? Didn't he see he had to let go of the past and give her a chance?

Whoa. Was she really thinking they'd have that kind of a chance? Did she want a man like him? Maybe it was the toe-curling sex that had her considering it.

So they were great in bed together. Everything else between them was a balled-up mess.

* * *

Sitting on the bed with her legs folded in front of her, Farren put down the book and gave up trying to stop thinking about Elam and Congressman Shay. Between the two of them, she was exhausted. She didn't want to go back to Shay's yacht. Not with Elam. She didn't think Shay would say anything with him in the room, but it would be dangerous going by herself, and she was afraid of confirming her suspicion. But what better way to get him to talk?

Farren checked the clock. It was after eleven. She'd come into her cabin after managing to avoid Elam all afternoon. At dinner he'd quietly brooded. Was he still worried he'd gotten her pregnant? Or was it her distant mood that bothered him? It disappointed her that she hoped it was the latter. If her distance bothered him, that meant he cared. And if he cared...

She shoved the thought aside.

Getting off the bed, she slipped on some flat black sandals that matched the black sundress she wore and hung the strap of a purse around her neck and shoulder. The sooner she had answers, the sooner she could go home and forget about Elam. She left the cabin. The salon was dark and quiet. She knew at least one of the team members would be keeping watch. That would make leaving the yacht difficult. But not, perhaps, as difficult as getting past Elam.

She walked slowly into the salon. Through the shadows, she saw his body stretched on the couch. His gun lay on the coffee table, outside his holster for easy access. She stopped near the table, the sight of him sweet torture on her heart.

Seeing his chest rise and fall with even breaths and his eyes closed in slumber, she struggled with a pang of affection. Giving herself a mental shake, she bent and lifted his gun without a sound, keeping her eyes on him as she tucked it into her purse. She hoped she could figure out how to use it if she had to.

Backing away, she tread silently toward the door, then took her time sliding it open. Outside, she stayed in the shadows while she listened for the others. She heard voices topside and inwardly cursed her luck. They'd see her.

But then the voices faded and she wondered if they'd gone to the other side of the yacht. She stepped to the stern, looking up and behind her. The flybridge came into view. No one was there. When she reached the dock, she started running.

She couldn't be sure she'd gotten away unseen, but if she at least got a head start, she'd have time to talk to Shay in private. The marina was still busy, which gave her small comfort. Her heart hammered as she searched for Imaad and his men. Down another dock, she made it to *Lucky*. The salon was dark. She stepped onto the aft deck anyway. The door was locked.

Climbing the stairs, she only made it halfway before someone called to her.

"Farren."

She turned and saw Shay standing at the stern rail.

"Edward warned me you were coming. He saw you on the dock."

She didn't know what to say.

"Follow me."

He went down the port deck and turned at a door that led below deck. Her heart sprang into alarmed beats. What if she was wrong about him? What if Haley's speculation was accurate and he was working with Imaad?

A Catholic anti-terror advocate?

It would be good cover. No one would ever suspect him.

He was American. A political figure who already had money. What motive would he have for aiding a terrorist?

She slipped her hand into her purse, gripping Elam's gun. She hoped she'd guessed right that he'd sleep with it ready to fire. At the bottom of the stairs, Shay walked down a narrow hall to the right. Dainty light fixtures on the walls lit the way past closed doors. At the end of the hall, he opened a door. Why was he taking her to such a secluded place?

She stopped in the hall.

He turned on a light in what she could see was an office. A spacious one. Still holding the door handle, he waited for her to enter.

"I don't want my wife to hear us talk," he said when she didn't move. "She already suspects something."

Her shoulders relaxed. She eased her grip on Elam's gun and passed him on her way into the office. Light polished wood paneling and bookshelves with tempered glass doors surrounded a desk and seating area. Farren sat down on one of the two white wing-backed chairs.

Shay sat in the other one, leaning forward and locking his hands between his knees, turning his head to look at her.

"Are you my father?" she asked outright.

He seemed to expect the question. "I don't know."

"If you're lying—"

He leaned back in the chair and held his hand up. "I'm telling you the truth. I don't know."

She leaned back like him and waited. She wanted answers tonight and wasn't leaving until she had them.

"When you came aboard that first time and told me Carolyn Fenning was your mother, I couldn't believe it was possible," Shay began, and she realized he'd accepted what she already knew. "She never told me about you. Why did she keep you a secret? If she'd had you with another man, there would be no reason to do that. I can't stop thinking about that. Why didn't she tell me about you?"

"How did you know her?" Farren asked.

He hesitated. "You have to understand. My wife…"

"Someone is threatening me for a lot of money. Your wife has nothing to do with this."

He found her eyes and she felt him probe for a reason to trust her.

"Please. You're my only hope of finding answers."

"I could lose everything if this gets out."

"It won't come from me. I have nothing to gain from your demise. I only want my life back." A life in Bar Harbor. Without Elam. She fought to keep the sting from piercing her heart too deeply.

"I met her a long time ago. We had an affair. I was married then, too, and at the time I didn't feel for Carolyn what I felt for Pauline. I ended it. It was years before I ran into her again. We struck up a friendship and it led to more. She confided in me about her husband. She was beginning to suspect he was lying to her. About business trips. About meetings he had at bars. At first she thought he was having an affair. But one night she followed him and saw him meet with a man."

"Who?"

"She didn't know, but she was afraid it wasn't legitimate. When she told me this, I began my own investigation. I cared for her a great deal. It was different from when we were younger. We'd grown since then. I was falling in love with her all over again."

"You loved two women?"

"I love Pauline in a different way. She's my anchor. My best friend. My business partner. Carolyn was… We were…"

"I think I get the idea," Farren said, not wanting to hear him tell her about her mother's sex life.

"What I found about Jared surprised me," he said.

"He's an arms dealer."

His brow crowded his nose. "How did you know that?"

"Elam and..." She stopped herself in time. "Elam found out."

"He's very resourceful. It's good to know you're in such good hands."

She didn't know how to respond to that so she didn't.

"Did he find you or did you find him?"

"We sort of found each other." She didn't see much point in lying. "He chased a man onto my chartered yacht and saved me from being kidnapped."

"He was after this man?"

"Yes."

"Imaad?"

"No, but Imaad is the one who sent him."

"Did Elam know about Imaad before he chased your kidnapper aboard your yacht?"

"No."

Shay took his time before saying anything. "It would seem he and I have more in common than I originally thought."

"You both fight terrorism," Farren guessed.

"Yes."

She believed him. "What did you discover about Jared?"

"Everything Elam did, I imagine. Jared used his shipping company as a front to broker arms deals his friend Betts didn't want to get his hands dirty doing himself. I know he was working a deal with Imaad."

"What kind of deal?"

"Small arms, but lots of them. He was planning to bring them across the Turkey border into Iraq, where a group of insurgents would receive them. But he was killed before the sale was complete. Imaad transferred the money as negotiated, but the goods were never delivered."

"Did Carolyn know about this deal?"

"I made sure she did. We were seeing a lot of each other by then. I didn't want her with Jared anymore. Especially after he found out about us."

"He found out? How?"

"He had her followed. When she came home one night, he beat her. Badly. Her face was black-and-blue and it hurt her to breathe. She should have gone to the hospital. Instead, I put her up in a hotel room and stayed with her. She refused to go to the police because she was afraid of Jared." Farren saw his fists clench.

"I had plans to expose Jared with what I had on him, but I was too late. I did hand over what I knew to a friend in Homeland Security. That's what got our government's attention on him."

Handing over information to a friend was less public. It meant there was less of a chance his affair with Carolyn would be revealed. "Was Jared aware you knew about the arms deal with Imaad?" Farren asked.

"It's possible. Carolyn knew."

"Do you think that's why he killed her?"

"Yes. I think they argued about it and he panicked. He may have threatened to do something to stop me and Carolyn tried to protect me."

"Did you know Carolyn was going to go to Bodrum?"

"No. I thought I had time to execute my plan to expose Jared."

"She knew you were coming to Marmaris."

"Yes. I told her."

"What if she learned something about Imaad? He might have known you were going to expose Jared. Maybe he intends to kill you for costing him so much money."

"Jared is dead. What threat am I to him now?"

"Imaad is still missing three million."

"But it's you he's after."

"Imaad is here, Congressman Shay. Did you know that?"

"In Marmaris?"

"He's on a yacht called the *Sea Minstrel*. One of his men chartered it in Bodrum and he sailed here for the festival. He's been watching your yacht."

Shay stared at her, alarm widening his eyes. No doubt he was concerned for the safety of his family.

"I thought you knew," Farren said.

"No. How would I know Imaad would come after me?"

"If he gets his way, he'll have his money and you. Think of the publicity he'd gain, with your prominent background." Imaad could make a loud statement by killing someone like Shay at something as public as an international yacht festival.

"If he was going to do something, why hasn't he yet?"

"He knows he's being watched."

"Who's watching him?" Then he shook his head. "Never mind. Elam is, isn't he?"

Farren didn't say anything, Haley's warning to protect the team echoing in her head.

"Who is he? Is he working alone or is someone helping him?"

"You may want to get your wife and kids somewhere safe," she said instead of answering.

He nodded after a moment. "I'll fly them home in the morning. You should go with them. I would hate to discover I lose a daughter to a terrorist."

"I'm safest right where I am." But she smiled at his concern and noticed more about him. His graying hair had once been dark. His hazel eyes might show similarities to hers. And she may have gotten her height from him. She didn't remember her mother being very tall. But then, she didn't remember much about Carolyn.

If Colin Shay was her father, why hadn't Carolyn told him? Was it to protect him? His marriage? His career? Or had she only been protecting herself and a life with a man who didn't want children? How sad that she'd never know.

"What would you have done if you'd known about me?" she asked Shay.

His brow gave a grim set to his eyes. "I wouldn't have understood why she wanted to give you up." He hesitated. "But…if she'd have told you. From the beginning."

The burden that would have been on him showed in his eyes and the time he took before responding. "I would have risked my career and even my marriage to make it right."

Farren fought the hope rising in her. "You would have gotten divorced and married her?"

"I would have done what I had to do to have you in my life. Maybe Carolyn knew that, and that's why she kept you a secret. She didn't want me to lose my career. She knew what it meant to me."

What if he was lying about not knowing? What if he was saying all this to keep her from getting angry and going to his wife? Then again, he might not even be her father. Only a DNA test could determine the truth.

"Well. It's late. I should go." She stood and so did he.

"When this is over, we'll get some tests."

He surprised her with the suggestion. "I don't want to cause you a scandal."

"It would be a worse scandal if I turned my back on you now."

Farren smiled. "Thank you."

He smiled back and that was all, which made her grateful. She wasn't ready for hugs and a see-you-soon.

She needed proof first. That and time to get to know him if it turned out he was her father. Time to forgive her mother, too. Maybe she'd never be able to do that, though.

She opened the office door. And froze.

In the narrow hall, Elam leaned his back against the wall, turning only his head to fix the laser intensity of his blue eyes on her. His legs were crossed at the ankles and his hands were tucked under his arms, biceps bulging. His unbuttoned black shirt revealed a swath of bare skin. He wore no shoes. Outwardly he appeared calm. Cool. But she could see the fire in his eyes. And he was furious.

He lowered his arms and pushed off the wall. Taking two strides toward her, he barely acknowledged Shay behind her. She had to force herself not to look away from the energy of that look.

"I believe you have something of mine," he said.

He must have heard her leaving. Parting the opening of her purse, she lifted the gun and handed it to him.

He took it, checking the mechanisms before shoving it in the front of his jeans. His angry gaze targeted her again.

"Do you even know how to use it?"

"Yeah. You just pull the trigger," she retorted, not appreciating what sounded like condescension.

"You could have hurt yourself."

She folded her arms and scowled at him. "I'm not that helpless."

"Don't ever do that again." The force of his tone revealed how much she'd scared him. "I would have come with you."

"I didn't want you to come with me."

Ignoring her, he gave a nod to Shay. Taking her arm in a firm but gentle grip, he guided her toward the stairs. She climbed ahead of him. In the upper salon, she spotted Travis sitting at the table on the aft deck, talking to Edward.

His arms were folded and the barrel of his pistol was resting on his arm.

He saw them and stood, saying something to Edward, who didn't look happy at all. Edward didn't get up. Travis put his gun in the back waist of his jeans. Farren walked between him and Elam as they made their way down the dock. She could feel Elam's anger the entire way. At the end of this dock, she saw Keenan leaning against the side of a closed kiosk, looking to his left and right as they approached. He fell into step behind them. They reached *Rapture* and Haley came down the stairs from the flybridge.

"Everything's clear," she announced, her tennis shoes silent on the deck, dark ponytail swinging.

"Good. Let's meet in the galley," Travis said.

She followed Travis there, Elam and the others behind her. Travis pulled a chair out for her and she sat, bracing herself for an interrogation.

Elam leaned against the refrigerator. Haley sat across from her and Keenan sat to her right. Travis stood behind her.

"Imaad *was* going to buy arms from Jared." She told them about the plan to supply insurgents with small arms.

"Without his money, he'll have a hard time pulling that off," Travis said, "especially now that we're onto him."

"He also may want revenge," Farren said, and all eyes moved to look at her. "Shay exposed Imaad and ruined his plan." She explained everything she and Shay discussed.

"Why not just kill him if revenge is what brought him to Marmaris?" Travis asked.

"Wouldn't it behoove him to have his money first?" Elam asked. "A congressman's murder will draw a lot of press."

"Which he'd love," Keenan said.

"Yeah, but would he want the press before he gets his money?" Haley asked.

Elam shook his head. "No. Farren coming here forced him to change his plans. If she'd have given him his money like he wanted and not come to Turkey, he would have killed Shay by now. But she's here and he's having trouble getting what he wants."

Travis nodded. "He didn't anticipate having to deal with Elam."

"Okay," Haley said. "What are we going to do?"

"I say we take him out," Elam said.

"I agree. It's time to end this," Keenan said. "The three of us could board the *Sea Minstrel* tonight and finish them all off at the same time. Imaad and all his men. There are only five of them."

"It's too public," Travis said. "We need to draw them away from the marina. Otherwise, innocent people could get hurt."

"I agree," Haley said. "But how are we doing to do that?"

Gazes met as each of them considered possibilities.

Farren lifted her index finger. "I have an idea."

Chapter 11

"No." Elam pushed off the refrigerator to stride over to her. "No way."

She looked up at him towering over her. "It's a good idea."

"I won't let you do it."

"Elam—"

"You're not posing as bait for a terrorist like Imaad." He glanced at everyone else. "I won't allow it."

She looked around, too. "Imaad and his men were watching when I got ahead of Elam at the bazaar. We can do it again, only this time choose the location to our advantage."

"I have to admit, it does sound good," Haley said.

"I can't believe this. I won't let you do it."

"Elam, you're being paranoid," Haley said. "She won't be out of our sight for one second. It won't be the same as last time."

"Besides, she'd have a tracking device on her like she did at the bazaar," Travis said.

"We'll be in control at all times," Keenan said.

Keenan's comment left no doubt that everyone but Elam supported the plan.

Looking down into her eyes, Elam backed away from the table. Farren stood from her chair and went to him, putting her hand on his biceps.

"I'll be all right, Elam."

His anger didn't abate, but he didn't argue. He turned and left the galley.

Late the next morning, Farren sat in the motorized dinghy while Elam maneuvered through the marina. He'd barely spoken five words to her. "Let's go" and "Get in" were pretty much it. His brooding reached past her defenses. It meant he cared, more than he wanted to care. He didn't like the plan, but he'd go along with it because his team outnumbered him.

They floated past the *Sea Minstrel*. A man standing on the flybridge saw them. He didn't move as they headed out of the marina, only watched.

The "crew" of *Rapture* had left for the shore before sunrise. Imaad and his men wouldn't know where they'd gone.

Farren kept looking behind them but no one followed. Elam steered the dinghy to shore when they came to a stretch of secluded beach. She searched the woods for signs of the others on Elam's team, but saw none. Not that she expected to. She knew they were lurking in the shadows.

Elam hopped out into the shallow water and before she could do the same, he swooped her into his arms. He carried her to a soft, dry spot on the beach and set her feet down. The mesh yellow sundress that covered her swimsuit and the pretty straw hat must have gotten to him.

She looked at him with a raised brow. "I could have gotten to the beach on my own."

He ignored her and returned to the dinghy for their

basket. There was no sign of the *Sea Minstrel* or any dinghy carrying the enemy. They hadn't wandered far up the beach and would be easily spotted if Imaad and his men decided to follow.

Farren spread out a blanket and then sat down with Elam. They ate strawberries and sandwiches and drank Perrier in silence. A sailboat passed their staged paradise, but no one appeared.

Elam lay back on his elbow, watching the sea and the length of the beach. He wore only swim trunks. So far she'd managed to keep her mind off his bare chest and legs. But her gaze wandered there now, soaking up the light covering of hair over smooth skin.

"Did you ever see the movie *Casino Royale?*"

"Yes."

"You did?"

He looked at her from behind his sunglasses.

"I'm shocked you watched a movie I watched," she said.

"It was a good movie. A little long. And the romance was a little too drawn out, but it wasn't bad overall."

"The romance was the best part."

He smiled. "You would think that."

She smiled back. "It was refreshing that they showed the guy's body. You know the part where he comes out of the water?"

"You liked that part, huh?"

"The older Bond movies always showed the girl in parts like that. Bond never took off his clothes. It was always the girl who was exploited."

"They didn't exploit Bond in that movie."

"They showed a lot of his body."

"Not all of it."

"They showed enough."

"Why are we talking about this?"

She shrugged, not wanting to tell him what made her think of it.

He chuckled. "Do you want me to walk out of the water for you?"

"No." She lay down on the blanket and looked up at the sky, folding her arms under her head.

He climbed to his feet anyway. She propped herself up and watched him walk toward the water. He walked in up to his chest before he turned and started back.

She laughed at his grin and the way he moved so lazily and slow. She wasn't sure if he was trying to walk like Daniel Craig, but it didn't matter. Elam looked way better.

Water dripped off him as he reached the beach. Smiling, he came down onto his knees and straddled her on the blanket. Saltwater dropped on her. She laughed.

"How was that?" he asked huskily.

"You're getting me wet."

His grin turned licentious.

"Oh, stop it." She put her hands on his chest.

He lowered himself all the way down on her, chilling her and heating her at the same time. He pressed his mouth to hers. She tasted salt and man. A sound came up her throat, a moan of pleasure. He deepened the kiss before lifting his head.

"Your teammates are watching."

He rolled onto his side, putting his head on his hand and smiling down at her. "There's a boat in the water."

She looked out to sea and saw a small motorboat just offshore. "Is it Imaad?"

"I don't know."

The plan was for her to wander off alone on the beach. But once Imaad and his men came ashore, Elam and his team would be ready.

The boat motored alongshore, too far away for anyone on board to be recognized, and disappeared from view.

"I don't think he's coming," Farren said.

"I don't, either." He pulled a handheld radio from their beach bag and put it to his mouth. "Travis, we're heading back. We'll meet you on the yacht."

Farren helped him pack up their things and got into the dinghy without his help.

"Why didn't they fall for it?" she asked as they headed back to the marina.

"I don't know." His jaw hardened as they came back to the marina. She followed where she thought he looked and saw that the *Sea Minstrel* was still moored where it had been. But *Lucky* wasn't.

Had the congressman left early?

She boarded the *Rapture* ahead of Elam and entered the salon. The rest of the team hadn't returned yet. She spotted a knife sticking in the paneling. It held a white piece of paper with black handwriting on it. Foreboding crawled up her spine as Elam passed her and yanked the knife free. He read the note and looked at her.

Just then, the other three entered the salon.

"We had company while we were away." Elam handed the note to Travis, who took it and swore after he read it. Haley and Keenan read it next.

"They must have seen Farren go to Shay," Keenan said.

Farren took the note from him.

Three million, or your father dies.

There were latitude and longitude coordinates written underneath that.

She raised her head and found Elam with her eyes. Imaad and his men must have forced him to reveal the reason she'd sought him out late at night and alone.

"We'll get him back," Elam said.

How? Imaad wanted money. Only she could give it to him. She went into her cabin and dug her token ID key out of her bathroom bag. It would give her a random code every sixty seconds that would allow her to access her account. She brought it in case she needed more cash, but she could also use it to transfer money wherever she wanted. All she had to do was find a computer and log on.

"Farren."

She turned to see Elam standing there.

"It isn't your fault."

"Yes, it is. If I hadn't gone to him, Imaad wouldn't have had a reason to use him against me."

"Imaad came here to kill him."

She bowed her head and stared at the token ID key in her hand. What if Shay was already dead?

"What are you going to do?" Elam asked. "Transfer the money and then go tell Imaad?"

"He wants money."

"And once he gets it, he'll kill you." He walked into the bathroom and reached for her hand. Cupping it in one of his, he took the key from her. She looked from their touching hands to his face. Sympathy mingled with strong determination in his eyes. He wouldn't let her leave the yacht without him. There was something arousing about his protectiveness.

"I'll get him back for you," he promised with a murmur.

"Elam…"

He moved closer, reaching past her to drop the key into her bathroom bag. Then he lifted her hat off her head and dropped it to the floor beside him. The way he looked down at her melted the rest of her resistance. Right now, she'd do anything for this man.

Burying his fingers in her hair, he gently pulled her

head back. She flattened her hands on his chest and parted her lips to take in more air, falling into his hard resolve and heated passion. He dipped his head until their mouths touched. His warm breath floated into her mouth. She breathed it inside her, wanting all of him inside her.

He curved his hands around her waist and lifted her onto the bathroom counter beside the sink. She opened her knees and he moved between them. He kissed her harder.

The yacht began to move. It wouldn't be long before they reached the location Imaad had given them, but Farren couldn't think about that now. She looped her arms around Elam's neck and kept kissing him.

"I can't take the thought of anything happening to you," he rasped. He kissed her neck. "Farren."

He was afraid of losing her to tragedy. But more than anything, he was afraid he cared too much.

He held her head with both hands and kissed her ferociously. She exulted in it, absorbed the full impact of his emotion.

"Farren," he rasped again, sounding amazed and anxious and urgent. It scared him to lose control like this.

She coaxed him to keep kissing her. With a gruff sound, he did, making love with her tongue. He dragged up the hem of her netted yellow sundress. Then his hands were on her, sliding up her legs.

She held his face while he kissed her, so lost in this passion that it made her dizzy. He pulled down her bikini bottoms, leaning back so she could bring her knees together to let it drop to the floor.

With heavy breaths, he pushed down his trunks and stepped out of them. She pulled the sundress over her head and let it fall to the floor, parting her knees as he stepped toward her.

He kissed her, roughly again and again, pulling the tie

behind her neck, then the one at her back. Her top dropped to the floor. He looked down at her breasts as he held her rear and pulled her to the edge of the counter. The tip of him found her. He pushed into her, kissing her long and deep as he did. Holding her firm, he pumped back and forth. The quick, hard rhythm drove her to an instant peak. She came with a cry that matched his deeper one as he did the same.

Farren kept her eyes closed and nestled her face next to his neck, aware of their breathing and the warmth between them. After a moment, he kissed her jaw and then her neck. He moved his hands up her back, a warm caress. She sank her fingers into his soft, chocolate hair and kissed his rough cheek. Her pulse slowed to contented beats.

He moved back and his gaze took hold of hers, his face showing no emotion. But she sensed he felt much the same as her right now. Confused. Unable to explain what this meant for them.

She slid down from the counter and went to dress in jean shorts and a white tank top. He found a pair of jeans and a short-sleeved shirt, which he buttoned after putting on his gun holster. They didn't say anything.

Opening the armoire across from the foot of the bed, he pulled out a black case and put it on the bed. When he opened it, she sucked in a surprised breath. Black polished components of his sniper rifle were neatly packed inside.

He glanced at her, his eyes hard. She folded her arms in defiance. Did he think she couldn't handle this side of him? It surprised her to discover she could.

Lifting the rifle out of its molded holding place, he attached a part on the end and a telescope on the top. Then he loaded the mean-looking thing. His hands worked surely and efficiently. The same hands that had held her bare bottom while he pounded into her. She would never understand why *that* appealed to her so much, hands that had touched her while making love now handled a deadly weapon. Maybe it was knowing those hands had saved her. More than once.

He left the cabin and she followed him to the sundeck, where Travis stood at the controls in the flybridge and Keenan and Haley loaded their pistols. No one seemed to notice the extra time it had taken her and Elam to join them.

A few minutes later, the yacht *Lucky* came into view.

"Go below deck," Elam ordered.

She looked at him. "No."

"Farren."

"Elam, I'm not a helpless female. Quit treating me like one!"

Travis looked over his shoulder, smirking. Haley often sounded like that with him.

"I don't want you to get shot," Elam said, pinning her with an unrelenting gaze.

She marched over to him and ripped open his shirt, sending buttons flying. He looked down at it and then up at her. She pulled his pistol out of its holster, then stuck her face close to his.

"If I have to, I'll use this," she said.

His eyes lowered to her mouth and the look in his eyes softened. He took the pistol from her and showed her the safety. "Keep this on unless you need to fire."

She took the gun back from him and went to a bench seat that would keep her out of view except for her head. Elam sent her a frustrated look and went to position himself on the sunbathing pad beside her, aiming the rifle at the other yacht. Waiting.

Haley and Keenan went to lower the dinghy into the water while Travis brought the yacht closer to *Lucky*.

"That's far enough," Elam said, sending Farren a pointed look. "I want to stay out of range of their guns."

Travis slowed the yacht but didn't drop anchor. "You ready?" he asked Elam.

"Yeah." He looked over at Farren. "Don't move from that seat."

"Yes, sir." She saluted him.

Travis disappeared down the stairs.

Elam glanced down at his pistol in her hands and then back up at her face before he peered through the scope on his rifle.

He watched the other boat. Imaad and his men were away from the marina and innocent people, so as soon as he had a clear shot, he could start firing. The team had wanted to take Imaad and his men out. Now they had an opportunity. She just hoped they saved Shay in time.

Two men holding automatic rifles walked along the deck, eyeing *Rapture*. Still, Elam waited.

The sound of the dinghy starting preceded Elam's first shot. Farren saw a man drop on the deck. Elam fired again. The other man dropped. A third man ran out of the salon and started firing at the dinghy as it raced away from *Rapture*. The bullets fell short of their mark. Elam fired a third time. The man dropped. His sniper rifle could shoot at a greater distance than the guns the men on *Lucky* used.

The reality of what she was seeing disturbed her. It wasn't like watching a movie. Those were real people Elam killed. She looked at his profile. He didn't flinch. He stayed still, watching through the scope, waiting for his next target.

The dinghy carrying Travis and Haley and Keenan sped toward the other yacht. Movement on the other yacht made her look there. She gripped the rail as Shay emerged from the salon, held by Imaad, who pressed a gun to his head.

Imaad yelled something in Arabic. Probably a threat.
"Elam."

Elam ignored her. Another man came out of the salon
and aimed an automatic rifle. He started firing at the approaching dinghy. Bullets sprayed the water.

Elam fired once and the man dropped.

Imaad swung Shay with him as he turned to see the
fallen man. Her heart flew with fear and worry. Would
Imaad kill Shay now? She glanced at Elam but he didn't
fire. He didn't move. Just watched. Aimed.

She looked back at the other yacht. Imaad had moved
Shay in front of him again. He shouted angrily at the approaching dinghy. Shay chose that moment to make a
move. He rammed his elbow into Imaad's sternum and
gripped his gun arm. They fought. The gun fell to the deck.

Farren glanced at Elam. He didn't fire. Shay and Imaad
rolled on the deck. Shay tried to keep Imaad from reaching
the gun, but the other man punched him in the face and he
fell backward. Imaad crawled toward the gun. Picked it up.
Rolled onto his rear. Shay tried to run for the stairs leading
to the swim deck. Imaad fired before Shay moved out of
Elam's aim. She watched in horror as he fell. Elam had a
clear shot now. He fired. A hole sprouted in Imaad's
forehead and he fell backward onto the deck.

The dinghy approached *Lucky*.

Elam didn't move from his position. He kept aim and
watched through his scope as Travis tied on to the stern of
Lucky. Travis climbed aboard and Keenan and Haley
followed. Weapons drawn, crouching, they moved toward
the open salon door. Then disappeared inside.

A flurry of gunfire sounded and then silence settled
over the sea. It happened so fast. The three reemerged on
the aft deck. Haley waved over at Elam. Travis and Keenan
lifted Shay and put him in the dinghy. He wasn't moving.

"No." Farren gripped the rail tighter and watched them race the dinghy toward *Rapture*. Just when she may have found her real father, would he be taken from her?

She laid the pistol down on the seat beside her and stood, still holding the rail. Elam put his rifle aside and climbed off the sunbathing pad. He went to her.

She turned from the rail and let him take her into his arms.

"He was shot low and to the side," he said.

A sob broke from her. She gripped his open shirt and dug her forehead against him. He didn't think Shay would make it. She heard it in his voice.

"They're here." He moved her back from him and searched her eyes.

"No matter what happens, you did what you promised. You got him back for me." He'd killed Imaad as soon as he had a clear shot. There was nothing else he could have done.

Elam's disagreement, his self-doubt, showed in his eyes before he grimly turned away and went to the flybridge.

Wiping her face, Farren jogged down the stairs and hurried to the aft deck. Haley climbed aboard first. Then Travis lifted Shay and Keenan helped him get him aboard. Elam started the yacht moving.

Travis laid Shay on the deck and Haley ran into the salon. Blood stained Shay's white shirt. Farren knelt beside him. Haley reappeared with a towel and pressed it on his bleeding abdomen.

"Is he alive?" She was afraid to hear the answer. She touched his cheek. "Colin?"

"He's alive, but he's lost a lot of blood," Haley said.

She leaned over Shay. "Don't you die on me now."

Chapter 12

Farren stopped pacing the plain and sparsely furnished waiting room of the Ahu Hetman Hospital when she saw a nurse approach. Haley stood from the chair where she'd been sitting. Travis and Keenan leaned against the wall to her left. Elam stood from the chair beside Haley and came to stand beside Farren.

The nurse stopped before Farren. "He's going to be fine. He made it through surgery and his vitals are very strong. We will keep him here a few days and he will then be able to go home."

Farren collapsed against Elam and fought the tide of emotion pushing tears forward. He held her, thanking the nurse.

"That's great, Farren," Haley said, rubbing her back.

Farren sniffled and leaned back. Elam's mouth curved in a slight smile, but it didn't reach his eyes. Sensing him withdrawing from her, she lifted up onto her toes and kissed him.

"Thank you." She smiled into his eyes.

He looked over her head at his teammates.

"You might have saved your future father-in-law," Keenan said.

Travis chuckled. "Better not corner him, Keenan. You know how he gets."

"Looks to me like it's time to give up on military women, Elam," Haley said.

Elam stepped back from Farren. "We need to get the yacht back to Bodrum."

"We'll take care of that. You make sure Farren gets home." Travis gestured with his head to Haley and Keenan. "Come on. We can make a minivacation out of it."

Haley waved at Farren and Elam as she followed Travis out of the hospital. "See you two later."

"We'll make sure your luggage gets to the Maritim Grand Azur Hotel," Keenan said. "Odie made reservations. You can stay there until you arrange to fly home."

When they left, Farren looked up at Elam. He turned from the door and didn't say anything.

"I'm going to wait for him to wake up," she said.

He nodded. "I'll go get your luggage. Save them a trip back into town."

She nodded, growing more anxious over his mood. Now that his mission was definitely over, there was nothing stopping him from leaving. She wanted to ask him if she'd see him when they returned to the States but refrained. She didn't want to be desperate anymore. This time, the man she wanted would have to come to her.

He started to turn. "I'll see you later."

As she watched him go, a weight descended on her heart.

* * *

Farren left the hospital after Shay's wife arrived the following day. The woman had stayed away since talking to Shay after he regained consciousness. He'd told her what happened. He told her about Farren. He also told her about Carolyn, too. Pauline hadn't taken it well, but she'd suspected something was wrong and that was why she'd hovered so close all the time. She'd been trying to learn what was wrong. They'd have a long road ahead of them if they stayed together, as Shay hoped they would.

Farren went to the Maritim Grand Azur Hotel. There were no messages from Elam. He'd checked in the same time as her, but she hadn't seen him. He was avoiding her. Withdrawing. Maybe he'd already left Marmaris.

Her flight left in four hours. He hadn't told her his plans. Along with the sting of hurt, she also felt a good dose of anger that he hadn't even said goodbye.

Rolling her luggage behind her, she left the room. As she rode the elevator down to the lobby, she wondered what it would be like to go home. She felt different. Emptier. If that were possible.

The elevator doors opened and she stepped out. Walking into the lobby, she passed the reception desk. Stone pillars lined the open gray-and-terra-cotta tiled area. Someone rose from a gray chair in front of a planter with a palm tree. She stopped when she recognized Elam.

Dressed in a short-sleeved black shirt and faded jeans and black boots, he looked more gorgeous than ever. Those captivating blue eyes didn't waver from her face, as he searched for any sign of her mood. She kept it hidden from him.

He moved toward her, taking the handle of her luggage from her hand.

"I'll drive you to the airport," he said.

"I can take a taxi."

"It's no trouble. I'm meeting the others at Osman's. You're flying from Bodrum, aren't you?"

"Yes." How did he know she was leaving today?

"Odie checked your flight for me," he said.

It was annoying how easy it was for him to predict her thoughts. She started walking toward the front entrance, holding the door for him to wheel her luggage outside.

He led her to a black sedan parked under the front entrance canopy. She sat in the passenger seat. He shut the trunk and lowered his tall form behind the wheel. Tension hummed in the small space between them. She was too aware of him, his broad shoulders that took up the entire width of the seat, his long thighs. She wondered if he wore his gun under his shirt.

He turned his head and caught her looking. She averted her eyes, watching the busy traffic on the highway. Elam did a good job keeping up with the crazy drivers, weaving or braking when necessary. Drivers here didn't follow rules. If there were any.

"Will you have any time off?" she asked. She didn't mean to sound leading. "I mean…will you have to go on a mission right away?" It still sounded leading. "Not that I want to… I didn't mean…"

"Travis mentioned something after he talked to Odie. Looks like I might be gone for a few weeks."

She nodded. So that was the way of it. He would go from one mission to the next and never look back.

"What about you? What are you going to do?" he asked almost conversationally.

"I don't know. I can't stand the thought of not working. Maybe I'll open an antique shop. I could fix up old radios and sell them there, too."

His lips curved into a smile. "That suits you."

She looked out the passenger window. They sounded like two people riding the bus next to each other. Who would guess they'd ever been naked together?

Minutes passed.

She looked out the window again. Strange, how this thing between them seemed so significant and yet she couldn't feel further away from him.

They rode the rest of the way to the airport without saying another word. Elam parked the rental and helped her with her luggage. After she checked in, he walked with her as far as he could.

Now it was goodbye. This time for real. No one was going to jump out at her and throw them together again. She'd probably never see him again.

He stood staring at her, as if there was something he wanted to say but didn't know how.

"Well...thank you. For everything," Farren said.

He continued to stare at her. Feeling more and more uncomfortable, she glanced toward her gate. She felt his hand on hers and looked at him again. He pulled her toward him. His arm laced around her waist. She flattened her hands on his chest as he bent to kiss her.

She stiffened. He moved his mouth over hers. She didn't want to feel the sparks he set off. But it was useless fighting it. She sagged against him and kissed him with all her heart.

After long seconds, he lifted his head. She could stare into those eyes forever. Reaching up, she touched his mouth with her fingers and then traced the line of his eyebrow and trailed her fingers behind his ear. She kept looking up at him, wanting to memorize his face.

I love you, she almost said. Her breath hitched with the shock that zapped her. She did love him.

And that's what made this so different from the other times men had left her. This time it was more than her zeal to procreate that was being crushed. Her whole heart was invested now.

Taking a step back, he reached into his back pocket and removed a business card.

Still reeling from her revelation, she took it from him. TES was printed on it along with his name and one tele-phone number. Nothing else. She lifted her eyes in question.

"In case you need to reach me," he said.

And she knew what he meant. The only reason he'd want her to call is if she had something to tell him. He wouldn't want her to call otherwise.

That hurt. How could he?

Struggling with the tightening of her throat and the sting of moisture in her eyes, she slipped the card into her handbag. She hesitated before lifting her eyes, waiting until she had control of her emotions. She welcomed the numbness that seeped through her. She took in the sight of him one last time. Then without saying anything, turned and walked to her gate.

Elam had deliberately scheduled a different flight from Farren's. Better to break it off cleanly. His flight back to Denver had left the next day. Now he was on his way back to Roaring Creek, and he couldn't stop thinking about her. He'd wanted to see her last night, but what would that have accomplished? He didn't want to give her false hopes and he didn't want to fall any harder than he already had. Being with her on a yacht was different from being with her at home in the U.S. They lived in different states. He had a job that took him all over the world. She had a life on a secluded island. They might as well live worlds apart.

He tried to imagine himself living in Maine, in her quaint little house on the ocean. Mixed feelings assailed him. The idea charmed him but also filled him with cold dread. They could have a real family life—whether he was gone a lot or not. He couldn't shove off the sensation that he could be happy there. With her.

But would she be happy with him?

Travis parked behind RC Mountaineering. Elam sat behind him in the backseat, Keenan beside him, and Haley in the front passenger seat. She and Travis had been awfully chummy on the ride up here.

Elam got out of the car and watched Travis take Haley's hand as they headed for the back door. She smiled up at him across her shoulder.

Entering through the back, Elam followed Travis and Haley through what once was a kitchen but now housed racks of clothes and outdoor gear. Odie rose from a chair next to the checkout counter across the room.

"Cullen's waiting downstairs," she said.

"Hey, Odie," Travis said.

Odie looked at Elam. "So is there going to be a wedding?"

Elam sent her a derisive smirk.

"Where is she?" Odie asked.

"He took her to the airport in Bodrum," Haley said. "He said he gave her his card." She looked back at him in distaste.

Odie laughed. "As if she's ever going to call you."

Elam regretted telling the team anything at all, but Haley had grilled him, and he felt that he had to say something to quiet her questions.

"You do realize, you're the one who's going to have to call her, don't you?"

"Nice to see you, too, Odie." Elam headed for the stairs

leading to the basement. To his right, the conference-room
door was open. Cullen sat at one end of the long table,
reading a news article. Probably the one about Congressman Shay and the terrorist attack that nearly killed him.
Elam had already read it on the plane. There had been no
mention of TES, only of a passing yacht and the people
who stopped to help him after his boat had been attacked
by terrorists. No names were mentioned. There had been
no mention of Farren, either. The press didn't know who
had stopped to help Shay, and Shay had claimed he didn't
know, either. He'd been unconscious, so everyone believed
him, though there had been a lot of speculation over how
deftly his rescuers had killed the terrorists.

"Elam." Cullen smiled.

The others filed into the room. Elam sat adjacent to
Cullen and began the debriefing, careful not to reveal too
much about Farren.

After the debriefing wrapped up, Cullen looked from
Travis to Haley. "I need the two of you to fly to Liberia in
three days. We've got a situation developing there. It'll just
be a recon mission. Gather some information and bring it
back. We'll decide what to do based on that."

"If it's just recon, I can handle that on my own," Haley said.

"Travis is going with you," Cullen replied.

She sent Travis an unmistakable glare before returning
her look to Cullen. "Why does he always have to go along
with me on missions?"

"Because he's good."

"I don't need a protector."

"I never said you did."

"Then send Keenan with me."

Cullen looked from her to Travis. "Is there a problem I
don't know about?"

"No problem," Travis said, turning his head to look at Haley. "I'm going with her."

"You don't have to protect me all the time. It isn't your job."

"It's Liberia, Haley. It's too dangerous for you."

"Too…" She fumed. "I can take care of myself!"

"I'm going, and that's final. If you want to argue, let's do it over dinner tonight."

Her mouth dropped open and she stared at him. "Dinner?"

"Yes. I'm asking you to have dinner with me."

"Well, aren't you the charmer."

"Will you?"

She folded her arms and leaned back on the chair with a jerk. "Yes. But only to argue."

Elam smiled. He'd always thought the two of them would make a good couple.

Cullen looked at Keenan. "I've got a team headed for South Africa at the end of the week. They could use a good spotter."

"I'm their man," Keenan said.

Cullen turned to Elam. "You're taking a couple months off."

Elam sharpened to full awareness. "Why?"

"That'll be all for the three of you." Cullen passed his gaze from Travis to Haley to Keenan.

The three rose and left the room. When the door shut, Elam tried to calm his anger as he met Cullen's gaze.

"I questioned Haley about you and Farren."

"And that's why you're making me take a leave?"

"I don't usually pull an Odie, but this time I'm making an exception."

"I'm not following you."

"Take some time off, Elam. Figure it out for yourself."

Elam could only stare at him. Was he trying to get him to see Farren? Leave him with all kinds of time on his hands to keep the opportunity open?

Cullen checked his watch. "I've got to run. Sabine is cooking dinner for her mom and dad tonight." He stood.

"I don't need time off."

"That's not what I heard."

"There's nothing going on between me and Farren. I can do my job. That hasn't changed."

"I have no doubt in your abilities, Elam. In fact, I'm sure you could do your job just as well if you were married. It's the unsettled state you're in right now that worries me."

Married? A cold chill froze him on the inside. "I don't want to get married. You don't have to do this. I'm fine."

Cullen stopped halfway to the conference-room door and turned. "I'm not asking."

Elam followed him up the stairs, where Odie waited at the front door. It was so like her to hang around and gloat. She smiled. "What are you going to do on your vacation?"

Elam wasn't in the mood for her teasing.

"Leave him alone, Odie," Cullen said as he left through the front door. Then to Elam, he said, "I'll call you."

Elam turned his back when the door closed, ignoring Odie, and strode toward the back door.

"What do you want to bet when he does call, you'll be on a quaint little island called Mount Desert?" she called to his back.

He slammed the back door and headed for the car.

"Sorry, Elam," Haley said when he got into the backseat. "He wouldn't stop questioning me."

He didn't say anything, not trusting his anger right now. Haley didn't deserve the brunt of it.

"Maybe you shouldn't compare her to Veronica," Haley

said. "She may look like a fragile spring flower, but she really isn't. How many women do you know who'd steal your gun and venture out on their own in search of answers?"

"She does have guts," Travis said as he started to drive.

Elam looked through the window and didn't respond. Mostly because it all rang true. Farren wasn't what she seemed.

One of her chatter binges filtered up from memory. She'd told him about a movie.

A person's strength isn't always obvious right away...

Had he underestimated her? Was he so afraid of losing another person that he'd closed himself off to the possibility of love? Farren had told him as much. Could he trust her to stay with him despite the demands of his job? He'd never given her a chance to show him she could. But that was the problem. He didn't think he could.

Chapter 13

Farren sat with the phone in one hand and Elam's card in the other. It had been almost eight weeks since she'd last seen him. She should call him. She'd taken a pregnancy test two weeks ago. She'd purchased two more and performed those, too.

There was no denying it. She still felt the same as she had then. Deliriously happy and morosely depressed. The thought of having a baby thrilled her to no end. The fact that it was Elam's crushed her. This wasn't how she imagined her life going. She wanted a husband to go with the baby.

She pressed each number into the handset, but stopped before the last one and then hit End.

She growled low in her throat and tossed the phone onto the table. "Why is this so hard?"

Because he doesn't want to hear from me unless it's to tell him I'm pregnant.

How humiliating would it be to call and tell him? The situation reminded her of when she was a young girl and she was awarded a part in a school play but didn't have the nerve to tell her foster parents. She didn't think they'd want to go. She told them at the last minute and they hadn't come.

A knock on her front door provided a welcome distraction. She saw Delphie through the peephole and opened the door. She'd kept a close eye on Farren since she'd come home from Chicago.

"I got a new shade of nail polish," she said, holding a basket with all the supplies necessary to do their nails.

Farren sat beside her on the top step of her porch. Delphie handed her the polish.

"It's dark blue."

"Isn't it pretty?"

"You go ahead. I'll keep mine pink."

As she started to work, a delivery truck drove up. Farren took a package from the driver and saw it was from Shay.

"He send you another baby gift?" Delphie asked.

Farren smiled as she sat down again and opened the box. She pulled out a baby name book and a pair of tiny white booties. There was a note, too.

She read it out loud for Delphie. "I hope you don't mind. I can't wait to be a grandpa."

They'd confirmed his paternity after he'd recovered. It was the one bright spot in Farren's life. Not only had she gained a father, she had two half siblings, too. For once something went right for her. Well, the second bright spot. The first was the baby.

"Have you told him yet?"

Farren sighed, knowing who she meant. "No."

"You're going to have to eventually."

"I don't see why. He doesn't want anything to do with

me. It would be different if he wanted something to do with me. But then, if he wanted to something to do with me, he would have never left in the first place. I dated a couple of men like that before. You know, the kind who don't tell you to your face they aren't interested? One was an accountant and the other was a cop. The accountant I wasn't surprised to find was a coward, but the cop…who would think a cop wouldn't have the nerve to tell me to my face he wasn't interested? Why do they have to blow me off like this? It's repetitive. Is it me? Is it something I do? Something I—"

"He has a right to know," Delphie interrupted. "It doesn't matter how he feels about you."

As always, the reminder that Elam felt nothing hurt. "Every time I try, I can't go through with it."

Delphie stopped painting her toenails that god-awful color and looked over at her with sympathy in her eyes. "Maybe you should just write him a letter."

"He didn't give me his address."

Delphie sighed. "So call him."

But Farren already knew she couldn't.

Elam left his house in Washington with a stack of unpaid bills. He couldn't stand being here anymore. Damn Cullen for sentencing him to so much time off. It was driving him insane. He couldn't stop thinking about Farren. He wondered how she was doing and was disappointed she hadn't called. That meant she wasn't pregnant. It disturbed him when he caught himself wishing she was.

He drove to the mall, where he had a P.O. Box and could mail his bills. It was just an excuse to leave his house. He'd already taken a trip to the Caribbean, but the beach had only enflamed his thoughts of Farren. He'd re-modeled his entire kitchen and met his neighbor for the first time since he'd moved here two years ago. She was a single woman five years younger than him. She talked a lot, but was nowhere near as charming as Farren. There was no point to his neighbor's chatter. It made him miss Farren and think of her with an expanding ache. *There was nowhere to go to escape her.*

Entering the mall, he walked behind two older women. One of them was talking nonstop. He smiled when it reminded him of Farren. Then he passed a Victoria's Secret store. Pinks and whites jumped out at him. He turned away in disgust. Everywhere he turned, Farren surrounded him.

He didn't have long to go before Cullen sent him on his next assignment. He'd made it this long. He could make it a few days more.

He dropped off his mail and headed back toward the exit. At the Victoria's Secret store, he stopped.

Turning, he faced the entrance. Who was he kidding? He was miserable without her.

She wanted babies. Soccer. Parent-teacher conferences. A real husband...

His heart rapped to a faster beat. Did he dare risk trusting her? Apparently, his feet did. He walked into the store. Lace and silk and the scent of perfume assaulted his senses. He tipped his head back and closed his eyes, imagining her. Her amber eyes full of passion. Her body wrapped in a sundress. Those high-heeled sandals. That pink nail polish....

God, he missed her.

So, why was he still running? Why didn't military women appeal to him anymore?

Because they never had.

The thought popped into his head. No military woman would satisfy him the way Farren did. He loved her femininity. Not that there weren't feminine military women, but he'd convinced himself it was the tougher ones who appealed to him. Face it. It was femininity that he craved. Farren's. He loved everything about her.

Love. Yes. He loved her.

What kind of coward was he for running? It was time to stop. Be a man and admit his feelings. Take the risk and give himself to her all the way.

He fingered the delicate hem of a frilly white confection hanging in front of him. A smile pushed up his mouth. He had to be crazy for leaving her.

"Can I help you?"

A young woman with black hair and curious blue eyes watched him.

"Yeah. I need something pink. And sheer." Something Farren could model for him. "Really sheer."

If he could only convince her what a fool he'd been.

Farren plugged a vacuum tube into the tube tester and removed it when it checked out good. She put it back in her newest vintage radio. The sound of a car pulling into the driveway made her look out the window. She didn't recognize it.

Standing, the smooth material of her floral skirt floated around her legs as she headed for the door. She tugged the hem of her matching V-neck sleeveless top and straightened the pink pendant that rested near her cleavage. Her bare feet padded over the wood floor. Opening the door, she heard her own gasp when Elam climbed out of the driver's seat, big and tall and more gorgeous than she remembered.

He saw her and smiled, his gaze taking her in from her toes to her face.

Smiled?

She stiffened as her defenses rose, wariness keeping her joy from burgeoning. She put her hand on her stomach. Did it show? Had someone told him?

He stepped up onto the porch. She tipped her head back when he came to stand close. His eyes held an amused sort of hunger.

"What the hell are you doing here?" she asked, wishing her heart wasn't racing with a ridiculous tide of love and excitement.

"I haven't stopped thinking about you since I left Turkey," he said.

She folded her arms in defiance, afraid to let herself trust where she thought this was headed. Afraid of how he'd react to knowing she was pregnant.

"Every time I see something pink, I think of you."

"I think you should go now."

"Every time I hear a woman talking nonstop, I think of you."

"Go away."

Instead of listening, he took a step closer and put his hands on her upper arms. "I'm sorry I left you the way I did."

She stepped back so that his hands slipped off her and swallowed rising emotion that threatened to make her desperate enough to rush into his arms.

"I didn't know what I was doing."

"What happened to change your mind?"

"My mind has never changed. I was surrounded by underwear when it came to me. I've been wandering around lost without you. I just didn't have the guts to admit it before now."

"Underwear." She began to tap her foot, anger brewing to life. "That's why you're here?"

"I'm here because I finally realized what an idiot I am."

"Is that the only reason?" Did he know?

"What other reason would there be?"

She didn't say anything and watched him glance down her body, then meet her gaze again. It was too early for the signs to show much, but his expression went slack with realization. His body went perfectly still.

"You're pregnant," he said, shock all over his face.

She spun on her heels and stepped inside her house. It was worse than she thought. He was still too afraid of a future with a woman like her. She wasn't a tough military type. She wanted a real family—a real husband. She turned to close the door.

With one hand, he stopped her front door from slamming in his face. She backed into her living room as he advanced.

"You were supposed to call me."

Her back came against the wall across from the entrance. He crowded her.

She put her hands on his chest and pushed. He didn't budge.

"What did you expect me to do?"

"Tell me."

"Really. And then what? You rush to my side to do the honorable thing? Marry me? Be a father to your unborn child?"

"Yes!" His fiery reply rang loud against the walls.

"What about me?" She shoved him harder.

He still refused to budge.

She growled low in her throat and pounded him with her curled fists. "You'd have come for the baby." Tears brimmed her eyes.

He let her pound him once more. When she stopped, he put his hand on the wall beside her head, leaning closer, his mouth dangerously near to hers.

"I love you," he said.

That stole her ability to find words. She just blinked up at him.

"I love you, Farren," he said again.

"No, you don't. If you loved me, it wouldn't have taken you two months to come here."

"I want to spend the rest of my life with you. If you want me to quit my job, I will. I'll do anything for you. You're all that matters to me. I'm sorry for not seeing that before now."

Farren just stared up at him. Was it true?

She started crying. "Someone told you about the baby. That's the only reason you're here."

"No," he said.

"I don't want to believe you."

"I'm nothing without you. I came here for you. *Only you*. You're all I've thought about."

Tears dripped down her face.

He kissed her.

She gripped handfuls of his shirt in her hands, wanting to believe but afraid to.

"It's true, Farren. I love you so much I'm crazy with it." He moved to kiss her jaw, her cheek.

"Elam." The last threads of doubt fell away. She heard his heart in his sweet declaration. She sought his mouth. He kissed her hard.

She threw her arms around his neck and took him deeper.

He eased away, giving her a series of soft kisses. "I can't believe I walked away from this."

"Oh, Elam." She met his kisses before drawing back to look up at him, happier than she'd ever been in her life. "You don't have to quit your job. That's part of you and it's part of what I love about you and I wouldn't want to change a thing about you. I worked with a girl once who made her husband quit his job and take another one and their relationship went down the hill. He started drinking and staying out late and had an affair and she wasn't happy and he wasn't happy and—"

He kissed her again.

Farren smiled against his mouth. But then he moved back from her. "Wait here."

Bemoaning the separation, she followed him to the front door and waited while he went to his car. He came back with a present wrapped in pink paper.

She gave him a knowing, coy smile.

He smiled back as he handed her the box. She took it and went to a white chair in her living room, sitting with the box on her lap. She looked up at him.

"Open it."

Carefully, she did, peeling pretty pink ribbon aside and tearing pink paper. Lifting the lid of the box, she parted tissue paper and lifted the delicate creation that lay folded inside.

Holding it in front of her, she looked through the material at Elam, laughing. Yes, she could see him through it. The man was incorrigible.

His smile turned into a sexy grin. "Put it on."

She didn't see the point. She might as well be naked. But Elam wanted to see her in it.

Standing, she kept the lingerie in one hand and went to him. Pressing herself against him, she met his gaze. "Are you sure about this?"

"Yes."

"I'm going to have your children."

"I know."

"More than one."

"Good."

"We might even have to get a dog."

"I like dogs."

She smiled. "Do you?"

"Yes. I want what you want, Farren. It scares me to death, but I want it. With you."

He meant it. Her heart warmed and swelled beyond what she could bear. She kissed him. "It scares me, too."

He folded her in his embrace and kissed her with more meaning.

Gradually, she drew back. "When you're away, I'm going to miss you."

His eyes heated. "I'm going to miss you, too."

"But when you come home…" She smiled. She beckoned him. Love burst and sparkled inside her as she extended her hand, telling him without words what would be waiting for him.

He took it and let her lead him toward the stairs. "I'm going to buy you lots of underwear."

* * * * *

**We'll be spotlighting a different series
every month throughout 2009
to celebrate our 60th anniversary.**

Look for Silhouette® Nocturne™ in October!

Travel through time to experience tales
that reach the boundaries of life and death.
Bestselling authors Lindsay McKenna, Cindy
Dees, P.C. Cast and Merline Lovelace join
together in a brand-new, four-book
Time Raiders miniseries.

TIME RAIDERS

August—*The Seeker*
by *USA TODAY* bestselling author Lindsay McKenna

September—*The Slayer* by Cindy Dees

October—*The Avenger*
by *New York Times* bestselling author and
coauthor of the House of Night novels P.C. Cast

November—*The Protector*
by *USA TODAY* bestselling author Merline Lovelace

Available wherever books are sold.

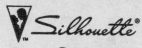

Romantic
SUSPENSE

**Sparked by Danger,
Fueled by Passion.**

The Agent's Secret Baby

by *USA TODAY* bestselling author

Marie Ferrarella

TOP SECRET DELIVERIES

Dr. Eve Walters suddenly finds herself pregnant
after a regrettable one-night stand and turns to an
online chat room for support. She eventually learns
the true identity of her one-night stand: a DEA agent
with a deadly secret. Adam Serrano does not want
this baby or a relationship, but can fear for Eve's
and the baby's lives convince him that this is what
he has been searching for after all?

Available October wherever books are sold.

**Look for upcoming titles in
the TOP SECRET DELIVERIES miniseries**

The Cowboy's Secret Twins by Carla Cassidy—November
The Soldier's Secret Daughter by Cindy Dees—December

Visit Silhouette Books at www.eHarlequin.com

SRS27650

Silhouette®
Romantic

SUSPENSE

COMING NEXT MONTH

Available September 29, 2009

#1579 PASSION TO DIE FOR—Marilyn Pappano
It's Halloween in Copper Lake, and someone's playing tricks. When Ellie
Chase's estranged mother is murdered, all the evidence points to her.
Ex-boyfriend and detective Tommy Maricci believes she's innocent, and
will do anything to prove it. But Ellie has secrets in her past, and she can't
remember what she did that night. Could she be guilty?

#1580 THE AGENT'S SECRET BABY—Marie Ferrarella
Top Secret Deliveries
Eve Walters's affair abruptly ended when she discovered her lover was
actually a drug dealer. Now, eight months later, she's pregnant with his
child when Adam Serrano walks back into her life—sending her into
labor! An undercover DEA agent, Adam is bound to protect Eve and their
child from the criminals he's trying to catch. But who will protect his heart
from falling for his new family?

#1581 THE CHRISTMAS STRANGER—Beth Cornelison
The Bancroft Brides
Trying to move forward with her life, widow Holly Bancroft Cole still
wants answers about her husband's murder. When she hires sexy but
secretive Matt Rankin to finish the renovations on her farmhouse for
Christmas, she never expects him to heal her heart. Except Matt is more
closely connected to Holly's past than either of them know—and once
revealed, it could destroy their second chance at love.

#1582 COLD CASE AFFAIR—Loreth Anne White
Wild Country
When pregnant Manhattan journalist Muirinn O'Donnell is forced to return
to her small Alaskan hometown, she slams right into the past she's tried so
hard to forget. Jett Rutledge doesn't want to see her either. They both have
secrets to keep, but as Muirinn investigates a twenty-year-old mystery,
danger sends her back into Jett's protective arms....